Each story in Andrew Bertaina's *One Person Away From You* is a shimmering monument to the lies we tell ourselves to get through the day. Seeing our own lies unfold on the page, the reader glimpses a world where we do not merely live and die alone, which might be Bertaina's greatest trick. His stories are that blend of invasive and cathartic that only seems to exist in worthy short fiction. Beautiful, somber, heartbreaking life in motion.

—Seth Borgen, author of *If I Die in Ohio*

One Person Away From You asks the big questions: of life and death, love and loss, God and nothingness. Bertaina writes with the mind of a philosopher and the soul of a poet. These stories are intimate, expansive, and wondrous.

—Jennifer Wortman, author of *This. This. This. Is. Love. Love. Love.*

With an enormous generosity of spirit crossing epochs of history, Andrew Bertaina's *One Person Away From You* offers prose poems, flash fictions, journalistic parodies, and fabulist histories that often begin with some premise or conceit from a known form, which they deflect or redirect, ingeniously insisting in subtle ways, "this isn't one of those stories." In one piece, a writer's new partner transforms a novel that was written before they met; in another an ancient map creates its own sea, in worlds where it's the imagination proves the determinant of experience, rather than the reverse. Masterful pieces include "A Translator's Note," "A Preface to the Third Edition," "Winter in the City," and "Maybe This Time." Bertaina's work continues in the tradition of Hemingway's "A Very Short Story" from *In Our Time*, but with a fabulist lens, and with a contemporary edge that incorporates Tinder, middle-class life, *Cosmopolitan*, and the movies into the fairy tale. I am so moved by this work, its intelligence and range, which is rivaled only by the tenderness and poignancy of the writing.

—David Keplinger, author of *The World to Come*

ONE PERSON AWAY FROM YOU

ANDREW BERTAINA

The 2020 Moon City Short Fiction Award

MOON CITY PRESS
Department of English
Missouri State University
901 South National Avenue
Springfield, Missouri 65897
www.moon-city-press.com

First Edition
Copyright © 2021 by Andrew Bertaina
All rights reserved.
Published by Moon City Press, Springfield, Missouri, USA, in 2021.
Manufactured in the United States of America.

Library of Congress Cataloging-in-Publication Data

Library of Congress Control Number: 2021945280

Bertaina, Andrew.
one person away from you: stories/
bertaina, andrew, 1982-

Further Library of Congress information is available upon request.

ISBN-10: 0-913785-95-4
ISBN-13: 978-0-913785-95-9

Cover designed by Shen Chen Hsieh
Interior designed by Michael Czyzniejewski
Text edited by Karen Craigo
Author Photo by Lauren Woods

CONTENTS

To my mother, who read to us
every night and instilled a love
of reading in me
that blossomed into writing.
(Sorry for all the profanity
in this book—I blame television.)

ONE PERSON
AWAY FROM
YOU

EVERYONE IN THIS STORY

This isn't one of those stories where someone has cancer. In this story, everyone has cancer. Everyone is sitting in a room with an old friend, while the sunlight fades behind a stretch of Victorians and old oaks, and the room goes dark and only the candlelight illuminates their faces, and they talk about cities in Eastern Europe that they haven't been to, but have seen in pictures and dreamed of like the invisible cities of Calvino. Everyone in this story is in a hospital room, watching the yellowed water in a vase of flowers—fat-headed sunflowers, bunches of pink yarrow, lilies, and sprays of indistinct white flowers with small, plentiful blossoms. Everyone is looking out the window at the rain falling fast on a brown hillside, pooling in the low places that used to be channels for a river. Everyone in this story is calling a loved one, or thinking about calling a loved one, and regretting the time they said they didn't love their mother, their father, the Mets, the Thanksgiving turkey, a family trip to Arizona; made an idle remark about the Grand Canyon being overrated, which wasn't even true. It was a wonder! Everyone in this story is sitting beneath a tree's yellow and orange leaves on a picnic blanket reading a story in which someone, maybe a child, has cancer, or a pig that needs to be slaughtered, or a dead parent, or a series of obstacles to overcome in order to achieve adulthood, which is, upon reflection, if the book went on, not all it's cracked up to be with the bills and mortgages and children who build train tracks and then abandon them without having once pushed Thomas beneath the series of intricate bridges. Everyone in this story is laughing at a GIF, warming a sleeping child on their stomach, waking up for a short swim, a long run, or to call someone who is living briefly in an Eastern European city. Everyone in this story is conflicted about the nature of their lives, wondering what philosophy to follow, what show to watch, thinking that they've heard good things about *The Wire*, but who knows, wondering what hobby to take up or start doing again, wondering about their wives and husbands, their children and their lovers, whether they've loved or been loved as they wanted. Everyone in this story just got a call letting them know that their life is going to end someday. Fuck. Fuckity fuck. Everyone in this story is taking the car in for an oil change, changing the light bulb in the garage, masturbating to a picture of an ex on Facebook, crying in the front seat of a car at a funeral, a wedding, stopping off on the long dusty road sheltered by a copse of trees and thinking about a day when they were very young and their father, now dead, took them to the zoo and held them on his shoulders when they were tired of walking. Everyone's father holding their chubby white legs as if they would never let them go.

SOMETHING MIRACULOUS

I'd been praying for something miraculous to happen, and yesterday seemed like it might be the day until my cat threw up on the floor. The glob of star-shaped food matted into the carpet made it hard to imagine anything out of the ordinary. Today, my cat was fine. She woke me by brushing her whiskers across my cheek, and we spent the morning lying in an aquarium of light.

I poured a bowl of cereal even though I didn't have clean spoons. The prize came out first, rattling around in the bottom of the bowl. It was a new spoon. I could tell that after years of failure things were turning around. The earth had shifted on its axis while I was sleeping and was spinning the way it was always meant to.

I read the newspaper but skipped the parts about children disappearing and fires burning near homes. I read a story about a man who saved a boy from drowning in the Pacific. Maybe life had been dirty and cruel because that's all we ever see. Maybe the world was like the surface of the ocean, where seals are flipped in the air by sharks but underneath lie symbiotic relationships of cyclical beauty.

I decided to start a magazine that would only report good things. It would have pictures of pets that had been found, not lost. Instead of pictures of kids with distended bellies, we'd have children playing baseball or eating a bowl full of rice donated by generous people who could possibly even be us. Our front cover would not say "45 Ways to Get Him Hot in Bed." It would say "45 Ways to Love the Beautiful and Unique Person That Is You."

I didn't know if the world was ready for my happiness, so I started sweeping the floor. Sweeping the floor has always made me sad because it goes back to being dirty so fast. When I was done, I put the broom next to the stove and called Sally, the only other woman who understood me. I told her that something miraculous was happening today.

While waiting for Sally, I looked out the window; the sky looked like a bowl of cream. The air was still, and the bases of the mountains were visible. Their black outlines rose into the clouds making a cap of light gray snow. I thought about how geologists find the skeletal remains of long-dead sea creatures on mountaintops and the millions of years it takes for the sea to recede and for the shifting of the earth's plates to turn a valley into a mountain. I thought that if we had millions of years here something miraculous would happen to us all.

Sally drove over, and I tried to let her in but the buzzer didn't work. It should have been my first clue that nothing was different. I walked downstairs, barefoot, in my bathrobe. The cement was cold, and one of the neighbors whistled at me through his window. I wanted to turn around and say, "Screw you!" But I didn't because today I was an integral part of a beautiful world.

Today, my neighbor was a really handsome doctor who worked daily on flattening his abs. He was single, modest about his good looks. He liked girls who lived alone with cats, which weren't always easy to find. Most men prefer dogs because they both hump indiscriminately. He wanted to tie me up on his bed so we could play "doctor" and have mind-blowing sex. He wanted to kiss me slowly on the spine first because he knew that's what I liked.

I tried to ignore the warm feeling that spread up my legs. I pushed the button, and Sally came in the rusted iron gate. She pulled me close and buried her nose in my hair.

"You smell like peaches," she said.

We walked upstairs together, but no one whistled. He probably thought I was a lesbian now, so I forgave him. I'm always forgiving men for not loving me. In the house, we sat and drank cups of tea. Sally complained about her ex-husband and started to cry. I held her hand in my own and whispered "Shhhh … shhhh," as if she were a child, and I was the wind drying tears.

I told Sally about the earth spinning in a different direction today. I asked her if she had noticed the change in the quality of light. I told her that I thought we were all underwater now, but because we weren't thinking about it, we were breathing just fine. It was like we were back in the amniotic fluid of our mothers, safe in the womb of the world.

"You're insane," she said, smiling at me anyway.

She had always loved me because I am a dreamer.

She looked at me. Her eyes were deep wells that I imagined swimming into, taking long smooth strokes through the emptiness of the iris until I reached the exterior, where I would lie on the white sand beach of her sclera as waves of brown sadness lapped at my feet.

Perhaps I loved her; it was hard to tell. I have always loved men and cats.

"If we're underwater, I guess I better start swimming," Sally said, lifting her hands over her head, pretending to swim the crawl. She turned her head to the side and breathed in on every third stroke. Her hair curled over her face, left a shadow on her cheek.

We laughed together, and Sally put her hand on my thigh. She leaned forward, and we started to kiss because she was the only person in the world who almost understood me. She wrapped her arms around my waist and then moved them up my ribcage, light fingers on my chest, a strange sensation of drowning. I pulled away from her and leaned back into the embrace of the couch.

We listened to each other breathe.

I smiled because I was imagining the doctor dropping hot candle wax on my stomach and touching the inside of my thighs with his stethoscope. I kissed her again, imagining him checking my heartbeat. We finished kissing, and I put away our cups of tea.

When I walked back into the room, Sally said, "Is that what you meant? Was that the miraculous thing?"

I looked at the space of carpet between us, the ocean floor—crabs scuttling on the ground, sea stars and sea anemones, thousands of things waiting to be touched. I knew that she wanted me to swim to her, so we could be alone on the island of the couch. I was still underwater; I did not have the breath to tell her that I didn't like girls, that I'd been imagining a handsome doctor, that I'd spent the morning believing in something beyond me.

So I told her I wanted to start a magazine, and that she could help me write articles that would help people change. I told her it was my calling.

"Is that what you called me here for? This magazine?"

I nodded because she wanted me to say a thousand other things that I couldn't. It doesn't change things, wanting to love someone because it would be nice to have a pre-warmed bed.

Sally stood and told me that we should go for a drive on the coast. She put her shoes back on and moved to the doorway. I swam after her into the morning light, walked across the shaded courtyard dotted with trash and the wreckage of children grown up, rusted toys and plastic buckets—the detritus of family life that reminds me of being alone.

We got into the car, and I wondered if I should tell her that I had made a mistake. Maybe I could learn to love her. She had thin lips, which weren't pleasant to kiss, but maybe I could learn to love them, too.

"Where are we off to?" I asked, trying to fill the silence.

Sally stared out the window at the sun, a blob of light over the ocean, spreading itself like oil on top of the water. "I thought we could drive by our old college haunt," she said.

And I thought how even in college Sally had probably liked women, but she'd never told anyone, how this was sadder than all the whales being harpooned by the Japanese. I remembered all those nights she'd listened to me talking about men, how bored she must have been. I put my hand on hers. "You're a good woman Sally."

She smiled, "A fat lot of good that's done me."

She drove down Milpas past the Hamburger Habit and onto the cracked side streets where all the Hispanics lived—chain-link fences, fading pastel houses, moms pushing strollers to the local laundromat. It felt like we were supposed to be there, driving into our past, that of the million places we could have been, God had chosen this one, and it was going to be OK.

"When you kissed me, did it mean anything?" Sally asked, her voice shaking a little.

I thought about telling her that in many cultures women kiss on the lips as a sign of friendship. And that I had seen my mother once kiss a female friend, their skirts lifting in a breeze. A brief brush of lips before the strollers went in opposite directions home—towards dishes, towards dinner, towards endless cycles of laundry and the smell of my father's cherry cigars wafting in from the living room. But I didn't know if that memory was real; it had the grainy quality of an old movie, of something I had made up.

"Look at how decrepit they've gotten," I said, pointing to the row of pink Spanish-style apartments where we'd lived on Salinas. Rust crept up the drains, and the sidewalks were pushed up by the roots of trees.

Sally turned the car in a slow circle at the end of the street, driving past the apartments again. I imagined the tidal wave that had come in the middle of the night and washed over these apartments. I thought about how water could invade every part of you but still hold you softly, like no lover ever could.

"It's been a fucked-up couple of years," Sally said, tapping the wheel with her fingers. "Who knew all the men in my life were going to turn out to be useless."

I wanted to tell Sally that life doesn't listen to you unless you grab it by the throat—how you couldn't want things to change; you had to make them. That's why I'd been praying for something miraculous, something to change.

"You've been like a godsend for me. Do you know that?" she said, patting my knee with her short square fingers.

She turned back onto Salinas, and we headed for Milpas. The sunlight crept through the clouds in a thousand different places like bits of water through a leaking dam.

"Have you ever seen Thelma and Louise?" she asked.

"No," I said, not sure where we were going.

"It's about these two women who are so messed up by men their whole lives that they start running. But no matter where they try to run to, it's more of the same shit. And in the end, they just say fuck it. The cops are chasing them for a murder they didn't commit, and they just drive off a cliff. It's a triumph, and it ends with a freeze-frame on the slow arc of the car, and you can just picture them both, sitting in the car for eternity, the happiest moment of their lives."

I told her that it sounded too sad. That they'd need food and water at some point and that they'd probably piss themselves and the car would become an unpleasant place to be. It felt hot in the car, so I rolled down a window to wave my arm through the air.

The men on the porches and sidewalks looked up as we drove, eyes following our movement in one dark line, as if we were prey on the Serengeti and they were tired old lions, incapable of chase.

We came to a stop sign. She rested her head on the steering wheel and started crying. A car beeped, and she put her foot on the gas without lifting her eyes.

"It's OK, Sally," I said. "I like Thelma and Louise."

She missed the next stop sign, and a pair of police lights flipped on behind us. "Shit," Sally said. She pulled the car towards the curb and shut off the engine. She looked at me intently, "Didn't you promise me a miracle?"

I nodded. I could tell that things were going to change. They had to.

A bead of sweat ran from her hairline down the side of her cheek. I held my hand back from wiping it away.

The police car stopped behind us and a tall officer got out. I watched him approach in the rearview. He walked with bow legs, spread out, all his weight on the outside of his feet. Sally turned the keys in the ignition and lead-footed the gas. The car's wheels were hung up on the curb and when she straightened it out the bumper banged back into the cement. The engine roared to life, the speedometer hit forty-five within seconds. Dogs behind chain-link started barking, and the children sitting on old red-and-yellow play sets watched with saucer eyes.

"What the hell are you doing, Sally?"

"I'm so tired. I don't know. I saw myself pulling over to the side of the road and doing what the officer said, taking a traffic course online to make sure I didn't get points."

"What's wrong with that?" I half-yelled, rolling up my window, which was blowing air like a jet stream.

"I could see myself, and you, just doing the same mundane fucking things over and over and over and hoping for change. Don't you want a real change?" she asked, facing me for a moment, her eyes pure liquid.

"Look at the damn road," I said, my body rigid. I grabbed the door handle and prepared for the inevitable impact. Sally whipped the car into the left lane and accelerated through a four-way stop. A car buzzed past, nearly broadsiding us. The faint sound of a siren started in the distance. She was up to fifty-five now, weaving through two-lane traffic on the main street. A police car appeared behind us.

"Where are we going?" I asked, over the roar of the engine.

Her eyes flipped to the mirror as she sped around a Suburban in the right lane and immediately cut it off to pass a Civic in the left. "The ocean," she said.

"Are we going for a swim, Sally?" I asked, but she didn't laugh. I was trying to remember that time we went skinny-dipping at night, how white her body was, if we'd touched. Maybe if I could remind her of this one thing, our fingertips beneath dark water, we wouldn't die.

The police car was gaining on us, and by the time we reached the on ramp, it was next to us. I could see the police officer's face, the sun making a blinding light off the black of his sunglasses. Then the impact as he rammed his car into the side of ours. There was a groaning noise as metal met metal and our car jolted up onto the curb. Sally slammed on the brakes as the police car flew by and over the train tracks before screeching to a halt. Sally threw the car in reverse and spun its smashed-up frame back onto the cement and towards the freeway.

The tires were burning and the car was making sounds like a dying animal. Sally's eyes were fixed on something in the distance—something only she could see. Maybe this was wasn't miraculous, maybe it was just today, the day I died without anyone ever really knowing me.

"Sally," I yelled.

Sally peered into the rearview and tried to put distance between us and the cop cars. My heart knocked against my rib cage as if it wanted to escape, as if it knew my shell of a body was about to be crushed.

"Do you remember that night we went swimming?"

The speedometer topped out at 140, but Sally kept flooring it. Plants in the median were a blur, but the ocean was a stretch of endless blue, broken by outlines of oil tankers. The tankers looked like pirate ships, warriors from a nation long dead, come back to claim the living. It was as if I were seeing the world for the first time.

Sally's eyes flipped into the rearview mirror frantically. "I've been swimming lots of times," she said.

I didn't remember what I wanted to say, words were trapped in my throat. I felt light-headed as if I were going to pass out. My body had stopped breathing; it had remembered that it was underwater. I wanted to remember what I was trying to say, so I closed my eyes, imagined myself as a toddler first learning how to swim. The cold hands of the instructor on my belly saying, "Kick, kick, kick," when all she needed to say was, "Breathe, breathe, breathe," and I would have been OK.

When I opened my eyes it was because Sally's hand was on my leg.

"We're going to be good together."

Behind us, a pair of police cars hovered like vultures waiting for the kill. I wondered if they would have to scrape my bloodied body off the cement, if certain instruments worked perfectly for the large intestine. I wondered if the officer who did it would be cute, if he had a family to go home to afterward.

I desperately wanted a family, a husband, a green lawn, so many damn things I didn't have.

We blew around a semi-truck driver who blasted its horn as we passed. The sound faded quickly, like the call of a dolphin. I could smell the rubber on the tires burning still. We had jetted through Santa Barbara and were headed up Coastal outside of Goleta, passing pickup trucks and small cars with surfboards attached to the top. A helicopter cast a shadow over the car.

"Remember our fingertips touching," I said. "Remember how we were both convinced that there were sharks."

The trees were a steady blur of green. The birds lifted from telephone wires and swam into the sky. I considered reaching for the wheel. But I could already see the slow arc of the car before it crashed into the sand below. There would be no freeze-framing for us.

"We're like Thelma and Louise," Sally said and touched my knee again.

So this is what it's like when things change, I thought. I knew I would have to find some deep well inside, deeper than the darkest part of the ocean where only the bleached bones of whales lie, picked clean by a thousand creatures on their long fall.

I put my hand on Sally's forearm. "Don't you remember the moon, Sally? The monstrous fucking moon, how we were sure it wanted to swallow us?"

Sally looked over at me; thick lines ran across her cheeks, her forehead.

"Look at the cars ahead of us Sally; they're split like the Red Sea."

I ran a finger across the back of her hand, tracing the spidery thin veins.

"It's a miracle. You can stop now. You can stop now," I said, sliding my fingers up her arm.

She started sobbing, and her foot eased off the accelerator. We drifted towards the side of the road. She pulled off into the dust, a patch of dirt, shaded by palms.

The ocean beat relentlessly at the shore below. The police cars rolled in behind us, officers got out slowly.

Sally looked at me with her deep brown eyes. "I love you," she said, as though it might still matter.

I wanted to jab my fingernails into her eyes. I wanted her to suffer because she had made me contemplate how little I'd done in the world. How I'd imagined sex a thousand more times than I'd had it, and how I'd tried so damn hard to believe that something beyond me existed. She looked out the window; I followed her eyes. The sea stretched out for miles, full of a thousand different creatures who had once been our neighbors until we'd crawled out into this miserable world.

Out over the sea, the clouds were dark; it looked like rain, like thunder, like all hell would be loosed on Earth. And I thought that if the world was going to stay the same cracked and broken place, if the bones of the dinosaurs were real, and all the dead were not going to rise from their graves to sing Hallelujah in unison, then something else was going to have to change.

So I pulled her head toward my chest as the police approached. I let her sob in my arms as if she were a baby and stroked her hair. "I know, I know."

COURTESY OF COSMOPOLITAN: 24 BIG BANG SEX TIPS

1. When, wearing a tweed cardigan, he asks after your afternoon, tell him of your love of Foucault. Talk about the nature of power and its role in structuring society and relationships. Use words like *patriarchy*, *maleficent*, *discipline*, and *punish*. Like most men, he will find this irresistible, and you're likely in for a wonderful afternoon of tepid sex followed by a quick shower.

2. Buy a blow-up doll off the internet. When he's out, pose with the doll in scenes reminiscent of a Rockwell painting. Post these pictures to Instagram. The doll should be middle-aged and mustachioed, and he's going to look best in themed outfits: baseball player, ship captain, dancer, etc. Above all, always keep the doll hidden when your partner is around. Finally, after weeks, take the doll with the two of you on a picnic, reenacting a pointillist painting with pink umbrellas, watery light, and the vague turquoise river running past you. If your partner is jealous, point out that he's jealous of an inanimate object. When he goes to sleep, pack your bags and fly to Vegas with the doll and take pictures of your wedding, after which you may have tepid sex.

3. Keep things sexy by surprising him after a shower wearing all your clothes. Dig through the closet and into winter clothes, putting on sweatpants and shirts that say things like JV TRACK on them. After seeing you, he'll be surprised and will probably want to talk about what kinds of times you recorded in the 400 meters.

4. Stand over him in the middle of the night, watching his chest rise and fall. If he wakes, startled, and asks what you are doing, tell him that you've been thinking about your 401K. Ask him if he thinks, in all honesty, if you're vested enough to retire at 57. Wake him periodically to help you with the math calculations. Like most men, he will find this irresistible.

5. Put on a pair of really baggy pajamas and demand to watch Netflix and eat Ben & Jerry's ice cream. If he says, "Tonight I just want to watch sports," remind him that only one of you loves sports, but both of you love to eat ice cream. It is so cold, so rich, and sweet.

6. Take up the art of origami. Fold him a swan or whatever people are folding these days. Tell him that the swan or whatever you happen to fold is a paper packed with meaning. If he asks, "Why did you make me a swan?" say, "All of life is an act of interpretation."

7. Read Tolstoy's *War and Peace* and talk to him extensively about the decisions the characters are making, the

possible impact on their lives and future happiness. Act as if they are real people, sitting in the next room, waiting for their lives to unfold like pages in a book while the tea steeps in the kitchen, leftover steam dissolving in the half-light creeping through white curtains.

8. Learn a foreign language. When your mother calls, use your new foreign language skills to speak in a tone that conveys complaint. Eye him significantly during the conversation and frequently shake your head in disgust. Remember, everything sounds like an argument in Italian. If he asks, say something in French, which will remind him of the bedroom because of all the episodes of *Red Shoe Diaries* he watched as a teenager in which French maids figured prominently.

9. Find a job that you are deeply passionate about. Prioritize the work; speak of it as something that helps you find meaning. Talk of your job often, taking brief breaks to reflect on what it means to make a difference in the world. Like many men, he will want to take up your passions and also sometimes have slow, sweet lovemaking sessions.

10. Make him a mixtape of your top all-time favorite songs from Celine Dione. When the one from *Titanic* comes on, move closer, fold your fingers into his, and say, "It's OK to cry," while making the sort of eye contact that

conveys deep sympathy, deep understanding. Crying is an aphrodisiac for most men, especially when they are the ones crying. If this fails, feel free to try Adele.

11. After his body has warmed the sheets, find a cool pocket for your cheek to rest on, and tell him about a morning from your childhood. Do not leave out any of the details: He wants to hear about the ducks, the rust-colored leaves, the musty scent of that autumn morning, the wind brushing away the drops of dew.

12. Sigh deeply and meaningfully when he comes to bed. If he asks what you are thinking, roll away and say, "Nothing." Then sigh again. Repeat this cycle until the repetition has washed over you completely and you are actually thinking of nothing. There are no dishes to be washed, no floors to be cleaned, no bills to be paid, no bosses asking for your progress on reports about Yemen. Let yourself fall into the moment slowly, like a snowflake from some very distant cloud; feel the immensity of the quiet.

13. Take up bird calls. As you are getting into bed, quiet him with a finger over his lips and repeat the slight hoo of a Barred owl. If he tries to speak, say, "Shhhhhh." Now is the time to walk to the window, to feel glass cool against your fingertips. Say, "If we are completely silent we might hear him." Call quickly, quietly, again and

again, the harsh net of the screen scratching against your face. "Are you out there? Are you out there?" When the owl doesn't respond, get back in bed and lie quietly. Do not begin sobbing. Everyone is alone.

14. Take up sailing on the weekends. Take the boat out over the water just after sunrise, when the light is green and the sea calm. Become an expert on sailing, listening intently to the lonesome cry of gulls skimming along the water as if they are harvesting the morning light. Speak frequently of your love of the movie *Double Jeopardy*, in which Ashley Judd is framed for murdering her spouse on a sailboat. If he asks what the plot points are, sit down with him and watch it. After the movie is over, discuss life insurance policies, saying that he's worth at least two million to you. Offer to take him sailing every weekend until he agrees. When you are finally out on the open water again, he'll take off his shoes and ask where you're sailing to, with a small grin creeping across his face. Hand him a cup of champagne that is drugged. As he slumps down against the siding, enjoy the quiet, the brine, and the slight breeze. Sailing was your thing. For a moment, you almost fucked that up.

15. Become a budding astrologist and deliver platitudes every time he walks in the door—be open to things, stay focused, today someone you love might be in need of you, someone you love may shut you out, be watchful, be attentive, today is the first day of the rest of your

life, be mindful, be. Eventually, admit that it's trash, but everything in life is trash, everything is just making things up until the day we die.

16. When the attractive waiter returns to the table to collect his tip, he will find bits of a poem scrawled on a napkin, something by Mary Oliver about the geese, the pebbles of rain, and the clear blue sky.

17. If you find yourself in need, talk to your lover about the philosopher David Hume. Tell your lover the truth—that despite all appearances to the contrary there really is no guarantee that the sun will rise in the morning. Let your bodies unfold in the eternity of the moment. Then flip on the television and watch an episode of *Bojack Horseman* that reminds you of despair, of cold gray winter days, of afternoons underneath a blanket that turn into quiet lovemaking and long naps.

18. Draw him a detailed picture of the people you love, not forgetting a single detail, but falling short just the same. Nothing in life is ever as easy as it seems. In the evening, describe to him what each line and a bit of shading on the page represents to you. Tell him what it means to have tried to capture something ineffable—an afternoon with your father on the lake when you were seven, his gray hair, his small quick hands on the fishing line or an evening spent with your mother when you were fifteen, or the precise tenor of the light coming from

a lamp as the two of you laughed and began to love one another again, as you had when you were a child. All your memories are like this, flickers of television shows that you watched in the nineties.

19. Tell him about your passions, the sorts of questions that keep you awake at night, lying in the darkness, while the world spins and spins and your mind tries to keep up with the awful pace.

20. Sleep. At all costs, sleep. When you wake, the world will once again be full of wonder.

21. Draw an elaborate map that has a pathway to your heart. Include everything that you've loved since you were very little: a kitten named Speckles, Jem and the Holograms, a math quiz that you got 100 percent on in third grade. Make the map like a maze with an entry point but no exit. This is the way, if I'm being honest, to Big Bang-type sex.

22. Read him a poem or a piece of literature that moves you deeply. After, sit in the quiet of the room and think together, sinking into the moment like a body into water.

"The universe is a solitary space, and all its creatures do nothing but reinforce its solitude. In it, I have never met anyone, I have only stumbled across ghosts."—E.M. Cioran

23. There are hours composed of uncertainty. The I of the morning is not the same as the I of the evening. I am perhaps immortal as long as I am I, though one day the I will be extinguished, at which point I will no longer be immortal. You and I are both abstractions, paintings hung on the wall of some very dark cathedral, in a land far away, where no one can speak our names. This is merely a longish way of saying, as some people are prone to, "In all things, if possible, be kind."

24. Come summer, board a plane and fly to somewhere in the East. If you can afford it, unmoor yourself even from the dock of language, float through the serpentine streets, ducking into cafes for cafe au lait, or slip into the church to beat the heat of the day, sweat dripping from your nose, and amidst the dark and cool stone admire a fresco of Christ's passion or Mary's lament by an artist whose name you don't know. And yet, there you are, face now tight with dried sweat, encountering their name on a wall, five hundred years after they have died.

Keep a journal throughout the trip and write briefly about the activities of each day, but spend the majority of the journal reflecting on how everything makes you feel, your impressions, your thoughts, the way that you connected to the fresco and the dead painter's name on the wall. When you return home, if he asks after the trip, the sunlight skimming through the windows, tell him that it is your own private journey, which you will talk about in due time. Say that if he sticks around for months or years perhaps you can begin to deliver bits and pieces of this trip, like glass washing up on the shore of some distant sea. In this way, we might achieve something like sex, or perhaps love.

FORTY DAYS

Brian Radkin died on the first day of November at the age of thirty-three in Colby, Kansas. He was wearing white overalls and installing a low-slope slate roof on the old post office. His body was stringy, like the clothesline that stretched across his mother's yard in Agra. He had blond hair that curled behind his ears and a tattoo on his right shoulder. Brian loved to smoke cigarettes: he loved to light one, hold it, and watch the lit end resting between his index and middle fingers. He would savor the taste at the back of his throat later; he loved the quiet moment he shared with the burning end first.

He stopped working, pulled off his gloves, hard hat, and earplugs, and put them on the roof. He bent, cupped his hand to shield the cigarette from the wind. The bitter weather suggested snow. He shook his left hand as if to warm it, dragged the smoke into his mouth and blew it out. His mind dipped back to his father's death, the cold white-tiled hospital room, a get-well balloon floating above the floor. He flicked the butt end on the slate and stepped on it.

Below him, people moved quickly through the cold, their boots crunching fall leaves. A delivery truck backfired in front of the general store; Brian turned, and his boots slipped down the side of the roof. He fell, fingers clawing at slate. His yell caused two women walking arm in arm to look up and witness his fall. He landed on the cement; a dog started barking; the wind blew in slow eddies; a stray balloon was caught in the branches of an elm, and lights began to flicker on down the center of Main Street.

The funeral was held on Sunday at the Episcopal Church—a large white building with a towering spire that cut across the gray sky—on the corner of Main and State. Gravestones lined the front grass of the church growing moss and collecting mold, and beneath the earth, bones waited for the flesh of the Second Coming.

Brian's wife, Mary, wore a black dress and veil. She entered the church to slow organ music, eyes lowered, passing the baptismal font on her way to the front pew. The pews were sturdy and dark, made of oak older than any of the congregants. The carpet was a deep red, and Jesus was suspended as usual from a wooden cross on the wall behind the altar; his head was down, a crown of thorns on his brow, no resurrection in sight.

The preacher—a middle-aged man with hard blue eyes focused on the back wall where thin light fell— prayed for the repose of Brian's soul. The low gurgle of a baby's laughter blended with the slow hum of the preacher intoning the liturgy. Mary sat next to her mother-in-law, Margaret, who sat ramrod straight and used papery thin tissues on her nose. Mary's eyes were dark and safe, half-closed slits of silt.

Light, refracted through stained-glass windows, fell in solid lines at Mary's feet; it was almost beautiful. Brian's fingers were curled in the casket; they were curled in her hair the morning after the wedding. They had stepped out of the small hotel, still fresh with love, into a rain falling sideways. They'd scrambled through quickly forming puddles and hidden beneath the boughs of an ash tree. A halo of sickish yellow light appeared in the sky, a sudden rainbow, which linked two masses of dark clouds. She remembered the cords of bundled muscle in his forearm wrapped tightly around her. They felt like staying beneath the dark and wet boughs of the ash forever, listening to one another breathe. The preacher went on.

"The Word was made flesh to slay death," the preacher said. "He became one of us in order to reconcile us to His holy will. So that when we die, we die in the hope of eternity. Not even one of the lilies of the field passes without His notice. How much more do you think He will do for each one of us? For Brian, who is now in the house of His Maker?"

Brian's body looked the same in the casket, lean and slender; his hair was slicked back, but no breath passed from his lips. Mary ran her fingers through the thin pages of *The Book of Common Prayer*. The wife of a dead man could scan the pages all day without finding comfort. She didn't want prayers; she wanted him.

Her mother had taught her to read from the Bible. Names like Melchizedek and Barabas had loomed large and unpronounceable against her finger, but she'd met Jesus there as well, not in a church like this, where slow arcs of dusty-looking incense traveled toward bits of sky trapped behind glass. She didn't put much stock in organized religion; as far as she could tell, the church was made up of people interested in sorting the wheat from the chaff when it wasn't even their damn job.

"But He rose again. His disciples did not recognize Him on the road to Emmaus; nor did Thomas, until he put his fingers in Jesus' palms and felt the wounds in His flesh. Nevertheless, He rose. He rose again so that we might all have the hope of eternal life. Amen."

The service ended with ladies in veils and muted lipstick singing of eternal life with God. The voices rose and fell in perfection, amongst all the dead things of this world.

Mary stayed silent, her lips murmuring unheard prayers. Did you really need him in your eternal choir? Don't you have enough bright things singing your praise? All I've got left is years piling into years. Still, people sang as if their voices could reawaken a hibernating God.

The reception was on the back lawn where no graves had yet been dug. Circular tables were set up on the grass, folding chairs covered in white tablecloths, the wind blowing stiffly, the thin sound of a baby's cry, people standing comfortably in their shadows.

The sunlight was plentiful and useless. A cold wind blew the tablecloths; only a framed photograph of Brian and Mary—taken on their honeymoon in Lawrence, his fingers curled in her hair, and her upper gums exposed in a smile—held them down. The men, mostly coworkers of Brian's, traded tears for afternoon liquor and talked softly with one another; their wives hushed children and looked askance at Mary, feeling sorry, happy to not be in her shoes. A few red leaves hung from a maple, and a gnarled oak stood above a sea of crumpled brown leaves. Mary sipped the drink in her hand, and she felt fingertips on her elbow and turned to find Harold. He was an old friend of Brian's—gray hair, a slight limp from some forgotten war.

"Mary. How you holding up?" he asked.

"Good as can be expected."

"I'm sorry." He took his hand from her elbow. The grass at their feet was yellow, turned by the first frost.

"There's nothing for you to be sorry about. You didn't slip off the damn roof."

He paused. A flock of white birds overhead, perhaps cranes, called out. They both looked toward the sky. Harold's arm lifted towards Mary, and she stepped out of his shadow. His fingers were left awkwardly grasping air. "If you ever need something, give me a call," he said, peering at the V shape of the birds disappearing into the horizon. "The snow is coming; it'll be winter soon."

"I'll keep you in mind," Mary said, closing the space between them and squeezing his hands.

Harold nodded; the lines in his face slackened. "I'm still sorry he's gone."

"The good Lord giveth and He taketh away."

The shadows of the trees stretched on the dried grass, dark halos on the green. Children began crying, and the liquor started to turn the men back inside themselves, and they were ashamed of their earlier tears, eager now for home. A few cars started disappearing from the dirt lot; a quiet settled down over the evening like a pall.

Harold made his way across the lengthening shadows to Mary.

"You need a ride home?" he asked

Mary shook her head.

Harold ran the calluses of his palms against one another; she was beautiful. "You sure? You could come over to my place if you wanted. I'm sure my daughter's got something put together."

How could he consider such a thing with her husband not even one day in the ground? Her mother had told her that men were born fools and that was the way they died. "I'd like to be alone for a bit. I appreciate the offer, though."

Harold nodded and walked toward the parking lot with the rest of the mourners. Mary watched them go; a long train of the living disappearing into dusky light. Her friend Cindy, tall and big-hipped, sat next to her on a bench as the cars faded. They sat in silence, and Mary thought of Harold at her birthday last year, eyes lost in drink, fingers on her elbow, watching her, a hawk on its prey.

"You spending the night here?" Cindy asked as she shifted to face Mary, legs now touching.

"I don't have a home worth going to," Mary said, picking up a dandelion, watching its seeds scatter in the wind. "I guess I'll watch the sunset on this plain ugly day. Pretend to see something beautiful."

"What are you hoping to find by staying out here?" Cindy asked, dropping her hand into Mary's lap, wrapping freezing fingers together.

"I guess I'd like to make it to tomorrow feeling a little better than today. You remember what the preacher said about those lilies in the field. Sometimes I wonder if He notices a damn thing."

Cindy pulled Mary close and hugged her tightly. "We're all going to help you through this, especially Him. Just don't freeze while you're waiting for things to change; it takes time."

Cindy stood—rust-colored light fell on her calves, making them appear somehow paler—and walked towards her car. Mary watched the taillights of Cindy's car disappear behind a field of bluish corn.

Mary crossed her legs and blew a ring of cold air. The sky turned violet, a barn darkening in the distance, the shapes of things swallowed by night. Time passed until even the barn disappeared; only the dark blades of a windmill remained. She remembered an evening, long past now, when they had lain in a field gone fallow listening to unseen owls hooting in the dark.

Mary walked home in the November wind, hard cement giving way to mud. The two-bedroom they had shared for eight years was a half-mile down an unlit dirt road. She reached home, fingers cold, mind empty.

She opened the door and put her jacket on the chair in the living room. She didn't turn on the lights; she lay on the cold and dusty floor, ran her hands across the oak boards. The moon slipped through the window and settled beside her. She unbuttoned the back of her dress and dropped it to the floor. She lay there, bathed in moonlight.

She had met Brian nine years earlier at a diner. He had come in from a steady rain and was wearing a sweatshirt, ripped jeans, and a beat-up hat. He drummed his fingers on the table, watching rain fall on cement. Mary poured him a glass of water and noticed the muscles in his forearm keeping time with the thrum of the rain.

He turned to face her and flashed a lopsided smile, a row of near-perfect teeth, something warm in his eyes, "How you doing, miss?"

"Some days are better than others."

"Ain't that the truth." The wind blew streaks of rain up and down the window—forming what looked like sentient shapes that broke apart in the next sudden gust—and pooled in the sill.

"You want coffee?"

"Bit of coffee wouldn't hurt. Sure. You got a minute to drink some with me?"

Mary's eyes lifted. "Are you that lonely?" she asked.

"No, miss, I just think you're that pretty."

Mary had flushed beet red; she sat at the table awkwardly, looked outside the window at the rain.

"You forgot the coffee," Brian said.

Mary started to rise.

He put his hand on her pale arm. "I'm going to forgive it this one time. Sit."

They were silent for a while; cold air passed through the window, filling the space between them, putting a chill into her toes. Mary got up and poured them coffee. They sat with their hands wrapped around mugs waiting for the moment to change. By the time the coffee had been sipped to the dregs and that same rain had moved to another window, they were laughing together about something that wasn't funny because it felt good to share something.

He appeared three days after the funeral. Mary was reading a magazine, flipping pages, passing the time before sleep took her. She heard footsteps on floorboards and looked up over the bridge of the magazine, the chipped polish of her fingernails, and there He was. He moved slowly across the room like some ghostly projection; the lamp cast His shadow on the floor. He knelt to take off his boots, ran His firm fingers through the worn laces. He looked up at her and smiled; she'd always hated the grime He tracked in.

Mary watched the curve of His arm, the slow indentation of muscle. "You can't be real. I watched dirt fall on your casket, watched it fall all over you."

He crossed the worn floorboards and sat on the couch.

She watched Him steadily, eyes as big and dark as the day she was born. She let the magazine fall in her lap, turned off the light.

"Why didn't we have any children? Maybe you didn't know you were going to be gone, but I've got nothing left to hold on to."

He brushed the dirt from the lines of His hands, ran them over the fabric of His jeans. A nervous gesture, she'd seen Him do it a thousand times. Maybe He had come back. She crossed the space between them and sat at His side. "Do you remember that first day when you stumbled in out of the rain?"

"You bet, miss," he said, moving a stray hair from her face.

"I'm already starting to forget," she said. "This house is so damn quiet now. She fanned her fingertips across His chest, felt the rise and fall of His breath. "Even dead, you're a good-looking man."

He lifted her; she smelled the sweat on His skin, briny and familiar. She trembled and felt a longing in her stomach she hadn't felt in years: butterflies. She shut off the light, and only the silent moon watched their skin become reacquainted, like blossoms appearing after a long winter.

Mary woke with the sun in her eyes, an empty space where His body had been. She put on her bathrobe and walked through the house, put water on for tea, watched cream-colored clouds roll in from the north. She waited until the sun was raised in the center of the sky before taking flowers to the little spot of land under which He rested.

~

Three weeks after the funeral it started to snow, a white blanket settling over the restless trees. Her annuals were buried in the first hour, violet and pink, gone for a season.

Cindy came by at three, her sedan blue as the sky against the snow. Mary opened the door; Cindy pressed a vase of roses dusted with snow into her hands.

"I don't suppose roses will help at all, but here they are anyway. Don't suppose they'll hurt anything, either."

Cindy sat while Mary brushed snow off the flowers. Her hair was curled behind her ears; she stood for a minute, in snow-white light, wondering what to do with the roses. What did one do with roses? Where was the best light?

Cindy looked at Mary, lost and confused, standing in the wan light of her living room, snow falling heavily on the sill. "Don't brush the snow off. It's pretty, provides a nice contrast." She rose. "Put them here darling," she said, guiding Mary to the coffee table in the living room.

Now, why hadn't she known where to put the flowers? Was it proof that He wasn't real, that the whole damn thing had been in her imagination? Should she tell her old friend, or would they ship her off to a white room with big blank walls? "Tea?" she asked, turning from Cindy and towards the kitchen.

"Sure, hon," Cindy said. Mary flipped on the burner, watched the gaslight, the flame rising in its tame circle.

The two women moved to the kitchen, sat at the table, waited for the whine of water boiling. Outside, the trees were groaning in the stiff wind like the sound of some train winding its way up a mountain.

"How have you been holding up?" Cindy asked, tilting her cup to sip.

Mary's hands trembled on her cup, splashing dark tea on the ground. "I guess you could say I've been better. What if I told you I'd seen Him again?"

"Seen who, darling?"

Mary bent to the floor and wiped up the small stain. How does one go about telling someone they've seen a ghost? How did any of them do it that first time?

"Brian."

Cindy's eyes turned to Mary and away from the red-winged blackbird preening in the old elm in the yard. "You sure you saw him? No ghost ever did a woman good except the Holy One."

"He wasn't a ghost. He stood right in the middle of this floor, took His boots off like a gentleman."

"You sure?" Cindy asked, her hands wrapped tightly around her cup.

"Not sure of much," Mary said, rising, the dishrag steady in her hands. "Do you believe it?" Mary asked.

"Believe in what?" Cindy said, her eyes lowered. The glassy surface of her tea rocked in the small space like a tiny inland sea.

"In Him, that He came back."

"Maybe he did and maybe he didn't," Cindy said. "Let's get some more tea and talk about something else."

Mary went to the kitchen, dishrag still in hand. Did Cindy believe her? What did it matter if anyone believed her? She had seen Him with her own eyes.

She returned to the table, and they talked about the change in the weather while snow fell on dark rows of trees.

When Cindy rose from her chair she said, "You be sure to call me if you need me. You will. Won't you?"

"I don't have anyone else, now do I?" Mary said

Cindy wrapped her arms around Mary and pulled her close. "I'm here," she whispered, squeezing Mary's arms.

Mary waited for her car to disappear before she went to the sink with the cups, dipped a sponge in warm water and cleaned the rims. Her hands were dry and cracked. What was the use of a miracle if no one was there to see it? One day didn't change much; it kept her hoping, but hope wasn't going to last forever. "Godammit," she said, breaking a teacup in the sink. The shards formed a mosaic in the basin, broken pieces, reflecting dull kitchen light.

She slid mittens over her sore hands, put on a jacket. The snow had stopped but wind shook flurries from naked tree limbs. Mary walked to the grocery store, boots sinking, carving a small path in fresh snow. She liked the freshly fallen snow, the yielding white. It felt as if she were some European explorer, come to this place for the first time. It was strange to feel good; she quelled the feeling, bent back to the path.

In the store, she went to the produce section and picked out a yellow squash. That man had loved squash; it had been his thing. Maybe He'd come back again tonight. Mary felt a hand on her shoulder and turned to the store owner, a big Italian man, dark hair and an angular nose.

"I'm sorry about your loss, ma'am."

"Thank you."

"You know," he started, glancing down at Mary, "I remember Brian from before he'd even met you. We used to—"

Mary stopped listening. Why was this man telling her about her husband? Would it bring him back? Would it change a damn thing? No, he was dead, and as far as she knew, dead was dead. No story could change that.

"I'm sorry," he said, pulling his eyebrows together sympathetically. "I just wanted to let you know I knew he was a good man. Let me know if there's anything I can do to help."

When Mary got home, she put the bags down and sat on the old couch. Brian had carried it home in his truck three years earlier. He had picked it up from the side of the road; they'd fought over whether to keep it. The argument had been settled by making love on the old brown cushions—warm summer light, bodies slick with sweat.

And somehow it still smelled like that first day, a bit of must, a hint of brine, His skin. It was as if He were still alive in the thin lining of the couch. She sank into the smell and slept. A soft knock woke her.

She looked through the peephole—a tall man, a hat shading his face, grocer's apron tied around his waist, two bags in his arms. Mary opened the door.

"Can I help you?"

"Got a little extra something for you from the grocer."

"All right. You new? Don't think I've ever seen you before."

"First day," he answered, brushing her arm as he put the two bags on the counter.

An electric shiver ran up Mary's arm. She turned to grocer as if she had been hit.

"Everything all right, miss?" he asked.

"Fine," Mary said, trying to put down the tingling sensation where skin had met skin. "You need anything else?"

"Bit of coffee wouldn't kill me," he said.

She knew she should ask this strange man to leave, but Mary walked to the kitchen and started the pot anyway.

The man sat easily at the kitchen table, legs crossed, fingers tapping on the table. He looked outside the window at the street—mud and dirt, dead flowers, a jackrabbit that appeared then disappeared. They sat in comfortable silence while Mary waited for the water to heat up.

He was handsome in a way that nagged at Mary. His gray eyes were almost hidden beneath the brim of his hat. She stood, pulling her skirt into place awkwardly, and brought the pot of coffee to the table.

"I take it you've heard about my husband?"

He nodded. He leaned back in the chair, feet resting against the edge of the table. "You think you can make it without him?"

A laugh rose unbidden in Mary's throat. "I don't suppose I have much choice about that."

The man sipped his coffee and smiled back at her.

Mary hummed a slight tune but stopped when she caught him laughing. She brushed the hair back from her forehead, pushed it behind her ear. Damned if she wasn't enjoying herself. It was good to finally be laughing; she could not remember the last time that had happened.

He finished his cup and pushed back his chair.

"You want another cup?" Mary said, her voice shaking a little. She did not want Him to ever leave.

"I've had enough," he said, taking a teetering step as though he were drunk.

"You're lucky you're walking," she said, smiling again, despite herself.

He put on his coat, turned to face her, told her she'd be all right. He slipped out the door into the oncoming dark.

Mary sat at the table sipping coffee. She wondered why she was missing some grocer she had just met, why it had been so comfortable to sit in silence.

She heard His voice again in memory, like some straw turning round and round in the same cup. She remembered pouring coffee for Him before at the diner. How could she not have recognized Him?

Wind rattled the freezing windowpanes like some visitor turned away from an inn at the dead of the night still searching for a place to rest. Mary closed her eyes, wrapped herself in memory, tucked His body around hers, fell into sleep.

In the morning, she pulled off the sheets and put them in the washer. She walked into the kitchen and sat at the table. The sun was blinding off still-melting snow. Children lined up at a bus stop, and a lost chicken pecked at worms in puddles. His cup of coffee was still on the table.

She left the table and walked to their room. She pulled a pack of cigarettes from the bureau on his side of the bed. Brian had always called it his "little vice." He promised her that he'd fix it before he retired.

"Can't fix a damn thing now."

She flicked his lighter on and lit the cigarette, took a drag and nearly vomited. By the time the first cigarette had become ash, she had learned how to drag the smoke in without choking. She lit a second.

The smoke drifted from her fingertips and disappeared into the wall. She sat on the floor, reached for another cigarette. She imagined herself in a cloud of smoke, furniture, and walls turning a sickish yellow.

She hadn't answered the phone in a week. The red light flickered incessantly, warning of impending doom. Her parents had called from Kansas City; she had listened to her father's voice while smoking a Winston. Harold had called again while she was taking a bath, bubbles that looked like rainbows between her toes. Bills had kept appearing in the mail, red letters that knew nothing of death.

Mary lay on the couch, some old record playing dreamy music, and she was wrapped in sound, between awake and dreaming. She heard a car's engine on the street, clawed her way back to the conscious world. It was Cindy, come to make sure she was still in the land of the living. Why couldn't the whole damn world just leave her alone?

When Mary opened the door Cindy smiled, handed her a coat. "You decide to stop using your phone? Take a brief trip to the last century?"

Mary shook her head, "I've been busy."

Cindy sat on the couch and gestured for Mary to sit across from her.

Mary sat across from her, looked up from wavering shadows on the floor and met her steady gaze.

"Listen to me, Mary; you've got a whole bunch of people worried in this town. You and I both know he's gone, and sitting in this house with all of his old things won't change that. I'm not here to tell you not to be sad. If you need tears, cry a damn river. But just cry them with somebody. Remind us every once in a while that you're OK."

Mary's hands were busy twisting an afghan. She looked past Cindy as she spoke, through a narrow break in the trees at the water tower gleaming silver in the sun. "He's not gone, though."

Cindy stood, walked over to the chair in front of Mary. "I know you're still holding on to him in your heart. Lord knows I miss him, too, but he's gone to a better place."

"He's here all right. It just makes me wonder, if heaven is so damn good, why the hell is He still wandering around here?"

Cindy lifted her arms to Mary's, encircling her in a warm embrace. "You've got to get out of this house every once in a while. It would be good to take a break from being alone."

Mary's dark eyes welled with tears, like some spade of old, just breaking beneath the dirt to water. "What if He comes back and I'm not here? What if I don't see Him?"

Cindy pulled Mary to her feet, smiled a small smile. "You can't wait around on him forever. If you don't get out of this house in the next couple of days, I'll have to drag you."

An hour later, Mary heard another knock at the door and rose to look through the peephole. Harold stood in the shade of the porch, turning a hat over and over in his hands. Mary opened the door and invited him inside. He nodded, stepped inside, put his hat down on the living room table. She sat on the old couch while he stood awkwardly, hovering near the chair.

"How are you holding up, Mary?" he asked, his eyes darting from the floor to her face.

"I'm able to watch one day turn into another."

He was nervous, and his hovering in the kitchen made her nervous, too. "Take a seat, Harold," she said, gesturing towards the chair.

"Thank you," he said, pulling the chair beneath him, sitting gingerly.

"Mary, I came here to ask you something," he said.

"I'm willing to listen," Mary said, trying not to smile. It was like watching a schoolboy wander across an empty room to ask for a girl's hand the first time. How was it that people got no better at this?

"I wanted to ask you if you'd come by for dinner tonight. Brian was a friend, you know, and I'd like to help."

Jackdaws were whistling at the edge of her hearing, and a train horn blared. "I'll give it a thought," she said. "I can't make any promises right now." She knew she should offer him tea, but she didn't want to.

Harold rose from the chair, his business done. He went to the table and put his hat back on. "I've got to get back to work. It's been a pleasure," he said, tipping his hat like some cowboy of old.

Mary walked him to the door, shut it behind his back. She leaned against the thick frame, sighed, "When are you coming back?" she said.

By five, the sun had dropped until its rays were only a memory, a leaf print on cement. Mary curled up on the couch and closed her eyes. When she awoke, He was standing in the living room. Mary looked up at Him with a blank expression. "If you're really coming back, it's time to stay. I got friends who think I'm going crazy."

"Mary, it's me," He said, stretching out his arms.

"I can see you, but I'm not sure I believe in you," she said.

"Come closer," He said.

He took her fingers, ran them across His palm. It was soft in the middle, calluses beneath His fingers. She slid her arms around His sides, felt the rhythm of His rib cage, expanding and contracting.

She woke up at three, chest heaving and ear lobe tingling. The bedspread was tangled with the sheet and pillows on the floor. He was gone for good this time. She felt it in the hollow space of her stomach, where butterflies would no longer fly. Maybe the whole damn thing had been some strange dream. Maybe that's all life really was.

"Lord, do you believe in me?"

She shut off the light, and moonlight pooled at her feet. She walked through the empty house, running her hand along the furniture and walls, feeling the shape of things in His absence. "I didn't even get forty days," she muttered. Mary pulled out a pack of cigarettes, lit one. She took a long drag.

"Ain't no use waiting for a dead man to come back."

THE ARRIVAL OF THE SEA

The inland sea was not always there. Neither did we always live on the slopes of these mountains. Ours was a relatively arid country, bone dry for much of the summer, which means that for as long as anyone could remember the depression between the two mountain ranges was made up of cracked clay, scrub brush, a century plant, or the occasional purple flower, rising up like a snake from a collection of stones and dust. Now we are often awake at dawn, contemplating the light on the water, the gulls skimming the air. We have grown used to the sight of rigging and sails as if they were the century plants and flowers of our youth.

The village we used to live in was a few miles from what is now the center of the sea. Sometimes, late at night, I'll think that I can see the tops of the houses or the steeple of the church. In truth, some mornings a bit of wreckage will come ashore, a footstool, or a plank from an old cabinet, and we'll gather around and try and discover who it had once belonged to. Usually, we can't remember, and we leave the wreckage behind to get on with our new days, our new lives.

The village was mostly wooden houses, small, homely places centered around a hearth, where the family could gather in the evenings and listen to grandfathers tell stories of misspent youths. The land was honeycombed with wells that we dug in search of water. We lived recognizable lives in our village—drinking late into the evening with our neighbors, talking loudly of our classmates or aging parents and swatting flies away from the rim of our glasses with dried bread as the sky turned purple then faded to black. We were untouched by greatness, and content, in so far as anyone is content, with the hardscrabble life we'd carved out in the valley between the mountains.

The sea came into existence shortly after one of the endless campaigns led by Alexander the Great across Asia. The great man himself stayed in our most prosperous inn, where it was reported that the goblet he drank from turned to gold. He went upstairs early, his hand grazing the wooden rail, leaving, according to legend, his fingerprints imprinted on the wood. And I sometimes still search among that wreckage that comes ashore, hoping to find proof of this legend.

That night, after Alexander had gone to bed, we gathered to discuss our lives and our talk shifted. We suddenly saw how faint our dreams had been, how petty our dreams. We understood that we had not lived the lives that we had intended to, and we could see it clearly now beneath the great light that Alexander shone upon us.

Alexander's men's tents were spread across the valley, and the sight of their campfires was like that of wondrous fireflies spread out against a tableau of darkness. By all accounts Alexander slept well and left early the next morning when the shadows of the mountains still lay over the valley. His troops started to cross, elephants trumpeting, and horses screaming—the air was golden with dust, and overhead vultures clipped the sky with their dark wings. Alexander, his mind already turning towards the next battle, stopped and, with a hand over his eyes, gazed at the surrounding mountains. He asked a general of his and a guide, one of our locals, to join him in a brief consultation. He pointed at the two mountain ranges on either side of the valley and said that he couldn't imagine, given what he'd learned from Aristotle, why a lake of some size didn't lie between these two great mountain ranges that encircled our valley. For he knew, according to observations in cities he'd conquered and turned to ash that water flowed downhill and should have made a great body of water in our valley. He could not see why, given the rainfall over nearby regions, that water did not exist. This perplexed him, and he asked our guide again if there hadn't once been a lake where his men now stood, in shards of reddish light, banner glistening, waiting for his next command.

Years passed in our small village after Alexander left. Our lives changed in the ways they do; wives and husbands were acquired and we began having children, minding them quietly, forgetting that brief time he'd been among us. We saw our dreams being realized, or, given what happened later, perhaps extinguished like the fires in the valley that morning, whose smoke stayed for days before disappearing out over the mountains. The world as we knew it continued to spin a familiar tapestry: birth, marriage, children, and death. And then our lives began to change in a way that we could not understand at first.

In Babylon, the city where his great dreams came to rest, Alexander called mapmakers together to crowd around his ornate bed, capped with dragon heads carved in gold, to help remind him of his campaigns before he'd fallen ill. And when it came to our valley, Alexander, in his wisdom, had his mapmakers draw a large inland sea between our mountain ranges. After his death and elaborate funeral, the map made its way to our village through some gift or another, and we put it up on the wall of the inn where Alexander had stayed all those years ago.

The presence of the map delighted us at first, and we nudged one another into tales of when Alexander had been there, when we'd all been much younger and perhaps happier, laughing now as the living still can, at the map he'd constructed from his false memory, and how even the mighty had fallen. We smiled at the obscenity of the large inland sea pressing up against the mountain ranges like a body to a lover.

We did not understand then the immense power of that great man, content as we were to drink and laugh late into the night. It was the children who discovered it first when they returned to our village with the hems of their clothes muddied. The children told us wild tales of water bubbling up from the center of the valley, trickling among the rocks. We couldn't make sense of their story, in fact, knew it to be false, and we blamed them instead for playing among the wells, which we relied upon for our drinking water and we beat the children quietly or sent them to bed without eating and listened for hours to their faint cries like the sound of gulls from a faraway sky.

A month or so passed in this way, the children, now sullen, or sneaking away at odd hours to visit the center of the valley. We tended to our crops, yelled occasionally at our husbands and wives and tended to things like normal. Since it was spring, a group of us went into the mountains in search of wild blackberries, thick, and ripe. We climbed farther up into the mountains, following a thin ribbon of trail that we'd cut in prior years, nearing the summit where a large patch of berries lay. By midday, our baskets were full, our fingers bleeding, but we decided to make the last ascent beyond the tree line so we could marvel at our village below. When we reached the rocky summit, we gazed back and saw the familiar sight of our village, the rows of houses and stripes of farmland. But, beyond that, beneath the wings of gliding birds, we saw what we thought must have been a mirage: a small body of water, shimmering in the distance, catching and refracting light. We stood there, arguing about the water until every one of us agreed that what we were seeing was water, though no one remembered it raining. On the way down, we talked initially of the crops, of the ways we could divert the water to make our lives easier. And underneath that, like a subterranean river, our thoughts moved to the dark contours of the map on the inn's wall, the water hovering over the place where our village lay.

For a while, we didn't share our findings with our wives and husbands, but we soon found that we could not hide it from them. We told them about the water, apologized to the children and kept up our planning to irrigate the crops. But something within us had changed. Now we gathered at the inn in glum moods. Over strong drinks, which we often now had beginning at noon, we recalled the dreams that we'd had when Alexander rode through. We began to see that they had not come true, or only in fragments, which did not satisfy us. Our children had left us or turned lazy, our husbands and wives loved others or had gotten fat and uninteresting. We had never gone to faraway cities and remade our lives, nor built anything significant. We were common people engaged in a common struggle. We looked uneasily and hopefully at the horizon as if a ship, sails billowing, were about to appear.

~

And then we waited. One late morning, when we'd been up all night brooding, the birds suddenly went silent. And we walked outside into green-tinged light, children tucked on our hips, eyes lifted. But we were looking the wrong way we realized as we felt the water on the soles of our shoes, saw it rising from the ground as if Moses himself had called it forth. Some of us started to run to the town centers; others listened closely. In the distance, we could hear the slow wash of water approaching us. An idea occurred to some of us, who ran to the inn and burned the map, hoping that this act could change everything back to the way it had been before. The wisest among us started packing things up, clothes, shoes, odds and ends—things that helped us identify who we were.

The water claimed the village in a matter of days. Some of us lost everything; others managed to cobble together a semblance of their life in carts that they carried up the mountain trails. Strangely, it seemed like no one brought enough to really remember who they had once been. It was in the years that followed that we discovered who we truly were—many wives left long-time husbands and moved in with men they'd loved, or they moved into a shelter and lived alone and happily. Our children lost faith in us after the arrival and started moving into the magnificent cities to the east. Others moved into the great inland sea on ships and plied the waters far from everyone they'd known before, waking before daylight to fish or search for shrimp, and returning their catch to fishing villages that sprang up all around the sea.

In the years that followed I wondered if the sea, like our true selves, hadn't been there all along, waiting for the right moment to reveal itself when Alexander finally had it drawn on the map. Last week, over drinks with my new wife, a quiet woman from across the desert, we watched the sea gently lapping at the base of the mountain. Soon enough, she and her children went to bed, and I sat all night, looking out at the sea, quiet and dark, while I contemplated all I'd lost. I listened to the mournful cry of the gulls screaming until sunrise, when the sea revealed itself anew, shimmering like the back of a great serpent, tempting me to move yet again.

WHAT I'D FORGIVE

What I'd forgive is having sex in the hallway, on the red oriental rug that runs from bedroom to bathroom. Above you, the pictures of Paris—a windmill, a cobbled street in Montmartre, Rodin's The Thinker, a flowerpot holding red geraniums, hanging from a wire basket along the grand boulevard—the pictures, striped by sunlight that falls through the maple tree and then the bedroom window come afternoon.

But I wouldn't forgive if it happened in the four-poster bed where we used to lie curved like prairie dogs warm in their burrow and watch episodes of *Planet Earth*. I'd lie on the pillows and talk to you in the voice of David Attenborough, whose gravitas was never more appropriate than when that female bird of paradise flew away, flitting off screen towards the sunlight piercing the tops of the trees, and the camera returns to the forlorn male, alone now, and Attenborough chimes in, "Sometimes, even your best isn't good enough." We laughed at his voice, so British, so wistful for that fat, dancing bird who'd spent all morning using a stick to sweep the log where he'd be doing his dance. At the critical moment, his tail feathers turn up like a peacock's, creating the illusion of an electric blue mouth, cartoonishly large, and he hops back forth on the log, deranged-looking, hopeful.

What I'd forgive is driving the Honda through the hot streets, past bikes that lean on garages, past small rectangles of lawn, past the oaks, dusty and tired in summer, to the restaurant where you can get margaritas for two dollars on Wednesdays before eight and eat a basket full of chips, crispy and fried, so perfect that you can't avoid shoveling them in like an addict and asking for a second basket before you've even ordered food, politeness be damned.

But I wouldn't forgive, mid-happy hour, with the overhead fans swatting ineffectually at the hot air, if you pushed back your bar stool and went into the bathroom and stared at yourself in that square mirror, smeared at the base by people like you, searching their crow's feet, the lines in their forehead, for some sign of their future, of who they were or might become, and then thinking about how we once tried to have sex in that bathroom, with the orange tiles and the wallpaper with a repeating theme of a cowboy in chaps and a ten-gallon hat, walking towards the swinging doors of a saloon. Remember how we tumbled onto the floor and how cold the tile was on our bare asses? Remember the children we were going to have named Autumn and Winter? Remember the trips we were going to take them on to the south of France and how we'd not care on the flight if anyone cut eyes at us as they sprinted around the plane, joyous.

What I'd forgive is you drinking tea from those small porcelain cups that your maternal grandmother gave you, with wisteria climbing the side of the glass. And you, waving away bits of steam as you look out the window at the city—a tableau of fast-food wrappers, shattered bottles, and bits of grass, green and ineffectual, a line of crows sitting on a telephone wire that quivers in the breeze, a drug-store bag blowing slowly through the street, until it comes to rest under a car's old tire. Where do all those plastic bags blowing through cities end up?

Remember how every time I'd make you a cup of tea, I'd walk from the kitchen and into the small dining room, asking if it was hot enough for you? You'd say no, and I'd lift my sleeve and turn, my arm stretched over the back of the kitchen chair, so you'd see my flexed triceps, and I'd ask whether that was hot enough for you. And you'd smile and tell me to make myself useful by picking up a chocolate croissant and leaving you to your crossword and Earl Grey.

What I'd forgive is driving down the highway where the speed limit is only fifty-five, to where the pines give way and the water meets the shore. And where you can sit on a stone wall, throwing bits of cheap bread to the gulls, their wings scything the wind as if it were hay. But not the way you used to rub in sunscreen, SPF 30, always doing it with your mind elsewhere, such that I'd return from the beach with burn marks, and the shape of your careless fingers etched around the burn.

What I'd forgive is a trip into the mountains, cupped in hillocks of light that appears through the mountains of clouds, the silver limbs of olive trees, and you, bending down in the trail to cup, like the hills and the light, my crotch, the sound of other hikers still fresh in the air.

Remember when I used to walk up the trail making bird calls? I held my hand vertically in front of my mouth as I imitated grackles, wrens, and crows, calls I'd memorized on the long nights you stayed out drinking with friends.

And you'd ask, "What type of bird is that?"

And I'd squawk back at you. And when you asked again, I'd shrug and say, "I can't make out a bird you're saying." And you'd roll your eyes, your luminous mother-fucking brown eyes. Later, we'd tumble into our hot double bed, with the down comforter still on, and we'd sleep like two overheated angels, shooting down after the fall.

I wouldn't forgive a damn thing, so stay here on the porch, and we'll watch the fireflies wink in and out, listen to trees clacking in the wind. I'll make tea. And we can sit and talk on these front porch rockers as the darkness shapes the world around us, about the fact that sometimes even your best isn't good enough.

IT SINGS

I constantly forget things. I leave for work with an empty coffee mug; I leave toothbrushes in hotel bathrooms; I leave our children's toys at playgrounds throughout the city. I lose my keys in the door; I lose them underneath couch cushions and in drawers. Sometimes, I lose them right where they are supposed to be because I am looking for them in my jeans or beneath the couch cushions. I lose my sunglasses, only to find them on top of my head. I'd be lying then if I said I remembered our first meeting well. In fact, neither of us remembers that day in detail. Instead, we've created a story about that day, a narrative that suits us. Which strikes me as appropriate—life is about generating a proper narrative arc.

Sometimes, over pots of cheap decaf, we'll talk about the morning we met. We'll search our memories to unearth what made that morning special. Mostly, we invent the details: You'll say that I wore a top hat and a purple pinstripe suit and that I juggled the silverware to impress you, dropping the steak knife on my toe. I'll say that you wore a red evening gown with epaulets and insisted that we dance the foxtrot before dessert, kicking off your shoes and pushing back chairs with your delicate, pale feet. You say that I told you I wanted to name our children George and Charlotte and that I planned on becoming an astronaut who would spend his declining years in a colony on Mars. I say that you were upfront about having chlamydia, though a mild case, that you picked up during that summer you spent in Venice at an artists' colony, painting gondolas drifting funereally through the canals. Here is what I remember—a dimple on your right cheek, rain threading its way through acres of sky, and a jacaranda tree, weeping on the pavement.

Our reality was more mundane than these fictions. Everything was simple. We spoke quickly and confidently, made jokes at the appropriate times, and left with smiles and a promise to meet again soon. It was as if we'd known each other for years—as if you'd already explained what a duvet cover was, how to buy eggs, checking each shell for cracks, as if we'd already stood at the edge of the car, rubbing our children's feet vigorously, removing all traces of sand. The rest of our relationship would be like slipping into wool socks on a cold winter morning.

Now you say that I am impatient, while you sip tea and wait for the clothes to dry. You say that a vacation doesn't happen by dreaming of swimming off the coast of Spain in seas silvered by the moon: It is about having a healthy income, budgeting for time off, and making reservations months in advance at places with continental breakfasts. I say vacations don't happen at all. You say I need to fold the clothes. We, like everyone else we know, haven't had sex in months. We need a vacation, I say, and you remind me of the trip to your parents' house in Pennsylvania as you refold a towel that I had folded like an amateur.

Once, years ago in Mexico, we heard a child say hello to the moon. Hola, luna. It nearly broke our hearts.

I know that you are right about vacation. You are always, insufferably, right. I wake early and track the prices of tickets to Barcelona mid-June. I buy a guide-book at the local bookstore and highlight pages. I listen to podcasts in Spanish, so I can avoid fish, which we both hate. I learn how to say good morning, and how to ask after people's children and pets. I speak to you in Spanish. I call you señorita and, sometimes, señora. I drink too much sangria and perform a rendition of the flamenco that I saw on television. The children laugh at such foolishness and briefly join in, prancing around the room like ponies on fire.

In the afternoon I image an elderly man sweeping the serpentine streets of Barcelona under a warm Mediterranean sun—the backs of his hands, creased by veins, covered in dark knots of hair. I have already started to travel there—taking part in an early siesta.

"Hola, luna," I say to you in the morning, and you look back at me with your uninterested eyes.

"Shhhh," you say. "The children are sleeping."

We are being dragged along through the current of time with only moments to grasp like rocks, to keep from going under. Stop being dramatic, I hear you say to the voice in my head.

I see your reflection, ghostlike in the window, and now I am watching you, watching me, watching the rain. I don't remember anything well. The act of love is an invention. You put your arms around my neck and lean into me. Your skin smells of soap and lavender. Shhh. Quiet, my love. The rain is falling in the garden—it sings.

MIGRATIONS

Long after I've left my own children to move back out West, I remember a morning from my childhood. My mother, sitting by the loom, the warm light from the window catching the red in her hair, tells me that my father is a bird.

"He flew away," she told me, "somewhere south for the winter."

I misunderstood the metaphor and at school that week I borrowed a pair of binoculars from my best friend. On Thursday morning, I feigned sickness, coughing and saying my head hurt, and my mother let me stay home. After the door had closed and the car rattled away, I took the binoculars from underneath my bed and into the living room.

All morning, I watched the maples and oaks that made up the perimeter of our yard, scanning the trees for any sign of my father. By one o'clock, I was tired and hungry. But then I saw a flash of black and yellow, like the colors on the Mustang that my father used to drive. I moved the binoculars slowly, scanning the thin limbs of the tree, and there, his fingers curled around the edge of a small branch, was my father, his chest puffed out, watching me, watching him. The moment seemed to last an eternity, and then suddenly he was gone. And I moved the binoculars up and looked at the clouds, like tiny wisps of hair or pieces of paper cut by a child, and then beyond them, to the purple haze about the foothills, searching, searching, not knowing then that I too one day would learn to fly.

ONE PERSON AWAY FROM YOU

Last night, I decided to become proactive. The cable had gone out and I was staring at the reflection of the lamp on the screen. I turned off the stereo, which had been playing Joan Baez for weeks, and put three handfuls of food in Oscar's tank. I decided it was time I visited you in New York. Even from a hundred miles away, I could tell you were excited. Your new girlfriend was not going to like it. But she could become a story we'd tell our children on a camping trip—ribbons of fire that lick the dark, burnt s'mores, sticky fingers—about how we'd almost lost each other.

I watched Oscar swimming through the food above blue pebbles. It seemed as though he would swim forever—small gills, fanning out to catch water—in his lonely universe of glass. I lay in bed touching myself absently, and someone started coming up the fire escape towards our apartment. I imagined that it was you, that I could hear your dress shoes, heavy against the grates. When you arrived, we'd have wild sex with the lights on; after, we'd lie awake and reflect on the aesthetics of a backlit clavicle and the island of shadow in the crease where hip meets waist.

You'd outline my body with your fingertips, gently sliding your calloused hands across my back, goosebumps rising to meet you. You'd nibble at my ear and whisper, "I'd forgotten how beautiful you are."

You wouldn't roll away from me and say, "No, like this. Like this," holding yourself between your hands.

At the end, your near-perfect body would be spread across the smooth sheets, the firm line of your calves lit by a small bedside lamp. I'd wait until your chest was rising and falling and we'd forgotten the miles of cement you put between us. I'd whisper, "I forgive you."

And even though it turned out to be no one on the stairs, it was only one person away from being you.

I rolled out of bed, and I was careful not to disturb your side of our expensive mattress, which still held the shape of your body. The living room was pitch black. It was too early for sleep, for the darkness of dreams without you.

I couldn't wake up anymore with your arm curled around my body, saying, "Shhhh. You were screaming."

I couldn't tell you that in my dream I had been pitch-forking my family, even my youngest brother, chasing them through the barn, armed with death. I'd tell you that something must be wrong with me, that I was incapable of intimacy, and didn't these dreams prove that I was crazy? But your eyes would already be closed, your breathing slow and even as wind passing through fields of wheat, and I'd know that I wasn't going crazy because you weren't scared that I'd pitchfork you in the middle of the night. I'd be able to sleep, leg wrapped around yours, warm from sleep.

I couldn't find the light switch, so I lifted the blinds and pressed my face against the glass of our window. One of our neighbors was getting undressed. She wriggled out of her jeans, her legs brown from weeks of afternoon sun. She slipped off her shirt, and her bra did not match her underwear. She looked out her window into the dark. She did not know that I was watching her, that she was no longer our neighbor but mine alone.

She closed the blinds after she was done changing, and I looked out over the street, at the shape of the darkness, streetlights—making pockets of light. I focused on the gray fog of my breath against the window.

I woke up to pee during the night and checked the light on the answering machine. It was not flashing, so I used a screwdriver to open the back and make sure the battery wasn't dead. I started worrying that all forms of communication had been severed because something catastrophic had happened in New York. I pictured you lying under a pile of rubble, looking up at a crease of blue sky, and promising yourself that if you stayed alive, you'd call that strange girl you had loved so much. I went into the living room and turned on the television, and I was surprised that it was working, that it had come back to life. I watched all of the major news channels, but nobody mentioned a disaster. You were still alive and having rough sex with your girlfriend.

"Fuck," I said, turning off the television. I lay with a pillow underneath my legs and thought about your brother. I tried to make you jealous by masturbating while imagining him naked, but you were too far away to care. I thought instead of how he visited us that first month and slept on the floor, and when we sat down to a breakfast of pancakes, he looked at you and said, "This one's a keeper." The crow's feet next to his eyes lengthened, and I prayed that you were listening to every word he said. You squeezed my thigh underneath the table, brief and softly, and the memory of your slender fingers on my skin helped me to sleep.

When I woke the next morning, I was a proactive person. I lay in bed for ten minutes, counting shadows on the walls. Five. The number of spider webs—long-abandoned—moving slowly in the air conditioning. Four. I wondered if the spiders were all dead or gone for only a season, like you. I wondered if you'd all moved out together and were living in a house of silk—filled with the husks of flies. It is a hard business being proactive.

Our neighbor's alarm clock blared through the walls. She pushed snooze three times before she got out of bed. I rose with her. In the bathroom, I listened for the thin sound of water on tiles before turning the nozzle. We took a shower together. I moved around the apartment with her, waiting for the bang of the cupboard so I would know when to have cereal. She slid open her closet door; it glided smoothly along the rails. Ours got jammed on the carpet, and I frantically tried to slide it back on track. I was afraid she'd leave me behind.

We looked into our closets together. We started to take our clothes off hangers and lay them on the bed. We both chose long skirts because it was too hot for pants. Hers was white, and mine was eggshell. We put on short-sleeved shirts with funny ties around the middle. They were in fashion because you said you liked them. We put on sandals, even though our toenail polish was too chipped to pull it off. I imitated all of her movements. In this way, I got ready for the day with our upstairs neighbor, who you always thought was beautiful.

I waited for her door to open before I stepped into the hallway. I fumbled with the key, and she almost got on the elevator without me. She was wearing a business suit. I looked at her strangely. Somehow, she had forgotten to wear a skirt. "Goodbye, Lindsey," I said when she got off the elevator in the lobby. She smiled back and nodded. She doesn't even know my name.

I took the Metro towards Union Station to buy a ticket to New York. On the way, I passed the woman with yellowed fingernails, the one who always asks for money. She was sitting on the cement in a pile of old newspapers. I didn't go home and look around our apartment for dimes and nickels so we could give her a dollar in change. I didn't start crying because the world is such a lonely and strange place. I didn't think about the last gray whale in the Atlantic, calling and calling into fathoms of empty water. Instead, I stepped over a newspaper that was collecting morning dew because that's the sort of thing you do when you're proactive.

As I descended into the warm mouth of the Metro, I rehearsed what I would say the next time I saw her. "I am in a bit of a financial bind right now. I really cannot afford to donate fifty cents to the homeless. But I'd really like to take you home sometime and introduce you to my fish." Maybe she'd think I was crazy; maybe I should just tell her about you. I bet she'd understand; we'd cry together as if we were from the same womb.

I was halfway down the escalator when I realized I was standing on the wrong side. A handsome man, wearing a business suit, brushed past my shoulder and said, "Excuse me." But I could tell that it was meant as excuse you. I realized that proactive people don't stand on the escalator; they march. So I marched down the stairs because I had somewhere to go. I wondered if you could hear my footsteps coming towards you.

I stood on the Metro, holding a metal pole. I didn't reapply hand sanitizer after every stop. A homeless man, with dirty gray hair, got on the Metro and said, "Cocksucking son of a bitch you better stop before I motherfuck you." I didn't worry that he was speaking to me, even though he kept pointing in my direction. I remembered what you said about everyone in this city being here only for a time, as if we are all stones tossed into the water waiting for the next skip.

The homeless old man got off after two stops and slipped into a stream of people. He was still mumbling, but whatever he said was cut off by the sliding doors of the Metro. I wish I had heard them. As the train moved on, his slumped form moved through the electric glow of the tunnel.

The train jerked to a start, and I thought about how wild your eyes got when we were having sex. I remembered the curve of your shoulder, the indentation where muscle meets bone. How you would close your eyes and burrow into my shoulder if it took too long. I wondered what other women you were imagining. Look at me. Look at me.

I missed my stop at Union Station because I was thinking so many things, the way as you move through the boundaries of a city, all the riders start to shift, the architecture of gentrification revealed on a metro.

I stepped off the Metro and thought about walking home, but it was my day to be proactive, so I walked to the other side of the Metro to go back to Union Station. The people on the other side of the platform watched me the whole time, probably thinking I was a tourist. "I'm not a tourist!" I shouted across the rails. A man on a cement bench across the way uncrossed his legs and looked up from his paper. Our eyes almost met.

I sat next to an old woman on my way back to Union Station. I sat carefully, keeping a fraction of space between our knees. She looked at me as if she wanted to say something—ask directions, or tell me about her grandson—but I turned and pretended to look at my reflection in the window. She sighed and tightened her hands over the bulk of her purse. She had a run in her nylon below the knee. Her dark skin trembled as we bounced between the rails. I found myself wishing our skins would touch.

I tried to imagine the thousand places her skin had been. I saw her on her wedding day: no veil, a tall preacher—who she would fall in love with after her husband died—helping them through the vows. I saw the afternoon thunderstorm and her dress, not bustled, trailing through puddles reflecting the sky. I saw her husband, watching television and blowing thin reeds of smoke. Her children, coming into the world and then leaving it with some person they thought they loved, the softness of her husband's hand stretched across the dinner table, a half-used wick with a flame that flickered between the ever-deepening lines in their faces. I moved my knee towards hers. She stood up to get off at her stop.

I exited at Union Station and put my hands on the railing of the escalator. I let the smooth black rubber slide between my fingers like a thousand people before me. When I reached the top, I stepped into the gray morning. Two bellhops were sitting on carts, trading stories, and smoke, and a line of people waited for taxis. I sat on a cement pillar, shaded by the building. A man slept on the ground, smelling of urine. Green-headed pigeons bobbed and weaved around a piece of bread as if they were boxers. Streams of people were running in opposite directions, and everyone looked as if they belonged. I walked towards the train station to buy a ticket.

I did not take the train to New York. I rode the escalator back towards the beating heart of the city that lived beneath the ground. I didn't take the train because you might have called or come back while I was gone. Maybe you were preparing dinner in the apartment we used to share. You had probably turned the stereo down and were listening for footsteps on the stairs.

I pictured you walking through swaths of rising heat towards the flower store on the corner. There would be a stack of irises piled on my bed; they were the flower you bought me on our first date.

"Iris," you'd said. "It's Greek for rainbow," and handed me the purple flower.

When I reached our Metro stop, I ran up the escalator. A brief summer shower had come and gone in the time I was below ground. It scared me that the world could continue without me knowing. Maybe you didn't even live in New York anymore, maybe I was dreaming. I walked back to the apartment counting weeds in the cracks of the sidewalk. Thirty-two.

I was hoping you hadn't left, but as I started up the stairs, I realized that I'd been picturing your face wrong all day. I'd forgotten the mole on your right cheek, and I stopped on the green stairs; you were not at home. You were still with your new girlfriend in New York, sleeping in the afternoon, streaked with sunlight and lazy after sex.

I spent the afternoon and early evening working on a crossword. You would have known a three-letter acronym for an Arab state. I didn't. I started writing a letter to you with every third word crossed out so you would remember that I'm interesting. I read the letter. It was inscrutable. It was night again, and I was alone.

The apartment smelled strange. I ran the garbage disposal and emptied the trash. I could not find the source of the smell until I checked on Oscar. He was floating in the tank, belly up, stomach distended.

I want you to know that our goldfish died; I killed him. Our neighbor flips on her light, and I can see across the darkness between buildings. For a moment, I stop writing. I watch someone who is not you, but it isn't the same. I think about the millions of telephone wires strung across golden fields, the ravens perched on the wires, waiting for something to die, all the wires that run the length of the Earth, and none of them are carrying your voice.

So I called you, and I pictured you picking up the line next to your girlfriend, swimming up from the acres of darkness you are buried under when you sleep. I had always wanted to skip with you, but you had left the water with a beautiful arc and flown onto some distant shore I could not reach. I could only call it from the distance. You surfaced without me.

When your voice croaked, "Hello," I waited a moment. I whispered, "I forgive you. I forgive you."

RIVER WALK

We were walking by the river on a cloudless night, half-drunk from an evening out. You took your shoes off as we strolled on the cobblestones, damp from rain. The night was cool, and eddies of wind stirred wet leaves, flapping half-hearted hellos. We'd left the bar so you could be home in time to say goodnight to the person you loved.

"Are you cold?" I asked.

You shivered and folded your arms beneath your chest.

"Wait," I said, taking your arm. I rarely took action in our time together. That whole summer on beaches, on trails, in bars, I had been like a small raft tugged along in your wake. I was waiting for you to turn into the light that night, waiting for you to say that you'd left him, or loved me, waiting for a moment that would shift our relationship. This was long before I knew that most of life is taken up by waiting, wanting, wishing away the quiet hours of any old day without hope of change.

"Come here," I said, and pulled you close.

Years later, a friend of mine told me that you'd moved to Indiana. I was living with a girl in Brooklyn with whom I was very much in love. My friend and his wife had your Christmas photo up on the refrigerator—two kids, a husband, and a retriever, tongue lolling. That afternoon my friend and I walked through the icy streets of New York, in a terrific hurry because it was so goddamn cold. The trees had icicles hung from them, like lights on the world's saddest Christmas trees. On the way, we talked about our jobs, office dynamics, and the people we'd once known. I thought of you, quickly, intently, while the snow flurried and scattered, muffling the sounds of the street.

Eventually, all afternoons in bars and all evening river walks will be forgotten. Our memories and minds will fade until nothing remains of us but particles from what were once human beings filled with possibilities. But we burn for a moment, and I remember pulling you underneath my arm that evening and the slight parting of your lips—the small smile of surprise that swam across your face like light on water.

"Are you warm now?" I asked.

And you smiled, still surprised, and said "Yes," briefly relaxing beneath my arm, the warmth of your body soft against my ribs, the water in the river dark, and the silver light of the moon tangled in your hair like fish in a net, like stars in the net of the sky.

THE EARTH IN ITS FLIGHT

In those days the Earth hadn't settled into the orbit that we're accustomed to now. The sun was in a slightly different place, which often caused problems in the Earth's orbit. These wobbles from the typical rotation would cause widespread panic and famine as whole swaths of the world would be on the dark side of the sun for months. Crops and animals died, and if that wasn't enough, the cold and the dark made people ferociously unhappy, and so they'd take up smoking or drinking, or with a stranger to try and cope with the crushing hopelessness of it all.

Meanwhile, the people who lived on the other side of the planet were bathed in perpetual light. And though they often started out feeling happy to be getting so much sun, and were tan, and worked long hours while still coming home and playing with their children, eventually the loss of precious sleep started to tear at them like a rend in a silk garment. First, they'd forget to pick their coat up from the dry cleaner, or they'd give the wrong denomination of gold at the general store. Eventually, the fact that the children never slept before ten p.m. would start to make them irritable, and they'd snap at them or at their spouses, whom they had once thought they loved. In some of the longer stints they'd start forgetting more essential things like the names of their mothers and fathers or household pets. And they'd walk around the neighborhood asking other people if they remembered the dog's name, which eluded them. There was once, during the longest stretch on record, nine months in the sunlight, when a soothsayer convinced everyone to walk around on all fours and pretend they were cats.

It was around this time, as I was sunning myself in a bay window, slipping between sleep and consciousness, that it occurred to me that we could not go on like this forever, drinking water from the fronds of ferns, and licking ourselves to keep clean when we all had perfectly functional baths, some even claw-footed or marble with nozzles and attachments to reach parts of your lower back that otherwise remained out of reach. People were kinder then, as old people are fond of saying, more ready to accept that the project of human existence was a corporate rather than an individual effort. This is not to convey that we sat around holding hands and singing spirituals, but I suppose it's true that the conditions, such as they were then, forced a sort of communality that you don't see now.

And so, after I'd lifted myself from the sill, from the stupor of a month chasing and chattering at flies, batting at balls and scratching furniture, I helped to guide the effort to change the way of the world we knew. Through a series of letters and men riding on horseback or skywriting in biplanes, we started all the able-bodied men and women to make a thick rope, a rope that we could tie together with knots, a rope so large that it would stretch around the world, so that we'd be able to hold the Earth in place when we felt it starting to shift, an act that would require the assistance of everyone in the world to pull desperately against the weight, to bear it, for a moment, in the tendons of their forearms, in the muscles in their back.

And I suppose this is a rather roundabout way of telling you about how I met your grandmother. We gathered together on a day when the Earth, according to the calculations of our scientists, who were much the same as scientists now: guessers. Well, we gathered that day to keep the Earth in orbit, and your grandmother was pulling on the rope next to me. Her stringy arms were blue-veined from effort, and her hair, the color of wheat at sunset, was tucked behind her ears. I didn't fall in love at first sight because no one ever has, but I knew for damn sure that I wanted to talk to her. After we finished pulling the Earth back into its natural orbit, sweat coating our shirts, stinging our eyes, I asked her out for a drink.

The road from the rope to the local tavern was dusty and reminiscent of a snake. On the way, she told me a story from when she was a child, hunting butterflies with her grandmother in the field behind her house. She remembered, or so she said, catching them in green nets and then holding them between their palms before releasing them back among the field of heather and coneflower and gorse.

It wasn't until she was nine or so that she discovered, during a lesson in one of her classes, that what they'd been catching in the field that day were dragonflies, not butterflies. And later she'd asked her grandmother why she'd called them butterflies? And her grandmother said that she'd loved butterflies, and she hadn't wanted to disappoint her, and so she'd turned the dragonflies into butterflies.

The wind was slow that day but thick. We felt it passing along our necks as we walked by the dusty trickle of a river. And your grandmother said that it didn't taint the memory at all to know that she hadn't been catching butterflies. Rather, it gave the memory a kind of color, something deep and pinkish, which she came to associate with love. She said, stopping for a moment, and catching my gaze, she said that she could see it around me when I was tugging alongside her, a pink aura hung around my narrow shoulders, a promise of things to come.

Of course, I fell in love with her then. I wasn't a fool, just young.

A PREFACE
TO THE THIRD EDITION

Dear Reader,

I am delighted to see the third edition of *A Man, a Sea, a Love* reissued for a third occasion this year. It is for my dear readers, intelligent, and kinder than I could have imagined, that I have modified this book as time has passed. The particulars of the novel have spun round in my brain often in the twenty-two years since its original publication; whole scenes and conversations often seem more real to me than my own life. Time marches on, bringing new perspectives, new insights, and, I hope, an improved version of the original text. The second edition made some minor copyediting changes and appended an epilogue, detailing the life of M. Plank and his wife, describing the birth of their two children and subsequent happiness.

The third edition, which I approve in full, introduces two small but important changes to the original novel as conceived. These changes influence both the structure and character of the novel, improving on it in ways that I could not have understood when the novel was first finished on that small property in southwest Missouri.

The acknowledgments have been slightly modified to reflect the changing circumstances of my life. In my thanks, I have removed the name of my second wife,

Jane, to whom I was married at the time of publication. Her name has been replaced by that of my third wife, Kristin. Though this change may appear minor at first blush. I believe, upon a close reading, that the change is important, as it was Kristin, not Jane, who is the animating spirit for the final successful marriage at the end of the book. Though Kristin was not present during the drafting, editing, and publication of the novel, and, in fact, though I did not meet her until five years ago, it is the image of an ideal woman, Kristin, that leads the narrator to finally cease his dissolute life and settle down in the colonial with the French doors, the small vegetable garden, and the library with a view of the river. Such a room, or settling into such a room, seems only possible with a woman like Kristin, and the acknowledgments have been modified to reflect this reality, and though I have not changed the words, I believe the spirit of the novel has been transformed by this small emendation.

The second modification, which was included after a long cold war with the publisher, the details of which are too sordid to get in to here, will no doubt come to the attention and perhaps confound even the most casual readers. The pages, 362-425, which in prior versions chiefly concerned the life of M. Plank and his courtship and affair with M. Santiago, are all now blank. Though on the surface this change seems, perhaps, silly, a joke, upon deep reflection, and a close reading of the novel, I concluded that those pages did not effectively depict the inner workings, the elliptical thoughts, and the artistic development of my protagonist during that time in his life. Instead of the inner workings of his soul, I'd mistakenly described frequent trips to the whore house, a series of drunken and debauched evenings in public gardens, and fits of love that leave M. Plank pleading from the ground floor of a moonlight square for M. Santiago to please approach the window.

These pages leave out the long afternoons the protagonist spent contemplating Gaudi's masterpiece, watching light gather at the apex of the Cathedral, Godlike. Nor do they account for the hours spent wandering the Barrio Gothic, skimming through the narrow streets like a skiff, peering down one of them at a sunset, in the foreground, the water glistening and a small tree leaning against a building. Nor do they describe a visit to the Palau Nacional, watching the reflection of that classic-inspired masterpiece ripple in a reflecting pool. It was these small moments in time, visits to art museums, contemplations of light playing on the underside of a tree, a woman's forearm dappled in light, mere ripples in the flow of a day that truly defined the artistic development of M. Plank, reshaping his relationship to the world.

However, rather than rewriting the text, which has always been, to my mind, in poor taste, I have chosen to remove the sections entirely. In doing so, I suspect that the perfect reader might sense the residue of the things that language fails to describe, the deeper meaning of those quiet months spent in the company of flowers, of water, of the poetry of life made visible after the dissolution of his first marriage. Somewhere, or so I believe now, lies the change that happens to him, which is the soul of this book, a change so profound that words fail me as they often have.

M. Phillips
April 12, 1978

ACROSS TOWN

Across town, my wife is on a date with another man.
And here I am, like a flower, gathering light in the
window and thinking of her. And just imagine that as
she reaches for her coffee or suddenly takes his hand;
imagine if she just as suddenly thinks of me, the two of
us miles away, lonely for one another.

IN THE GARDEN

As a child, I loved most the English ivy that climbed around the stone wall that encircled the garden. Ivy is an insidious thing, which grows until it is Lord of all. And yet I loved it, loved the way it crisscrossed the bricklike thoughts of a mind before sleep, loved the way it reddened in fall, loved the way its vines clung desperately to the crumbling brick, as I clung to afternoons then, wishing for them to last for days.

And yet, at the periphery of my childhood there lurked a quiet fear. I was afraid of many things: swimming, darkness, silence. I sensed something dangerous that lay just underneath the unknown. I spent a great deal of my early childhood outside in the company of my brother. He was older, and after a time these afternoons were spent alone, sitting on the grass beneath the boughs of an oak with streams of dappled light falling around me, the smell of violets carried by the wind. And just as I'd find myself sinking into the moment beneath the calls of songbirds and idle croaking of crows, I'd be gripped by an intense dread until I found my mother. Such fears are commonplace in childhood, I suppose, and I would have put them behind me but for a summer's day in my youth.

I was eight and full of hope for the things to come that summer—the hours my brother and I would spend together, the soft note of my mother's voice as she baked in the kitchen. I would lie on my back beneath large banks of clouds and imagine my future against the blue of the sky.

The garden was partially shaded by a row of chestnuts, and the sun's light was feathered by the leaves. Inside, our mother was watching television and paying the bills. My brother and I were throwing a small racquetball in the garden, bouncing it off the wall and chasing it down like dogs hunting a fox. I loved this game and my brother as I loved nearly everything then—cars, trains, the sound of a plane overhead, crab apples gathering afternoon light. My brother had outgrown most of our games, and I didn't see him as much as I'd like, so these afternoons together in the garden filled me with joy.

My older brother cocked his leg and wound up, imitating the pitchers we'd seen on television, dramatically kicking up his leg before sending the ball ricocheting off the stone wall, ping-ponging off iron tables and rusted chairs, skittering beyond the purple flowering vinca and into a corner of the yard where the ivy held sway. The vines were like corded rope, the leaves plentiful, rich, luminous, and green. Most days, we tried to avoid this spot by stacking chairs in the way, as it often took us half an hour or more to find the ball, but we'd been careless this afternoon.

This portion of my memory is hazy, but I believe my brother went inside to get lemonade, leaving me alone in the yard, sifting through reams of ivy to find the ball. Suddenly, or so it seemed to me, the sun tucked behind a large bank of clouds, and I was standing in a well of darkness. And I felt, as I had many times before, the presence of something foreboding that nearly sent me scurrying inside. And yet, doubting my unrest, which had always proved unfounded, I returned to the task and stepped into the small space created by my outstretched hands.

Beyond the ivy, I saw something inestimably strange— where I usually saw the vestiges of a stone wall I saw a hole instead. And, more astonishing, through that hole I saw a little boy, peering exactly as I was, searching for something lost. The two of us made eye contact, startled, and then we both dropped the ivy. I ran inside to find my mother, but she shooed me away, putting her palm over the phone, and I was left alone with my fear.

I never saw the other boy again, but the image of him, my mirror, my shadow, has lived with me ever since. I think I saw him on my wedding day and at the funeral of my estranged father. But each time I was sure he was there, it turned out to be nothing more than a distant cousin or the play of a tree's shadows on the wall. Yet he has lived with me ever since, stalking the quiet moments of my day.

And so I lay in bed that night, as I have almost every night since, wondering what the little boy who looked exactly like me was searching for. Was it a blue ball? Or was it something else that had escaped him? And underneath everything I do lies the quiet fear of my childhood, grown with me, like ivy on a wall. Every time I board a plane, or walk down the street, I expect to look up into the eyes of a stranger and find that it's him, ready to take up my life where I left off, repairing the relationships I've fractured, rekindling the loves I've lost, living, on this side of the wall, the life I thought would be mine.

WAKING DREAMS

We were at a holiday party on Fifth Avenue, which was lined with cute federals, and gingko trees that painted the streets in yellow, leafy walkways. The houses all had wraparound porches, some with swings, overhead lamps, rocking chairs. On the drive over, my boyfriend and I had listened to Joni Mitchell and idly chatted about the day. He drove slowly, as the roads were rimmed in ice and covered in brown slush, an early fall snow.

The party was an old tradition the two of us kept without knowing why, a gathering of people we'd met as graduate school students, he as a mathematician, I as an aspiring writer. Since then, our lives had diverged from those of our friends, Frost's old forking path. We hadn't changed our circumstances much. We remained in the same one-room apartment we'd shared during school and were still dating. In fact, it felt as though we hadn't changed at all. Though we were slightly sadder, I suppose. We hung our coats in a small closet, which smelled of mothballs, and entered into the fray of Christmas music and smiling people we half-recognized. It was a shame we weren't drunk on arrival.

Everyone else at the party seemed to be married. They were canvassing real-estate markets, talking about load-bearing walls and the cost of renovating, about finding a kitchen table made from chestnut, about putting in open kitchens. They were reviewing crime stats on their phones, discussing new coffee shops or neighborhood bakeries. They were talking of home brewing and future housing projects involving smokers and bay windows.

Some other people had children. The children weren't there, and the people seemed to be wishing after their children, looking anxiously at their watches, scrolling through their phones to find photos of birthday parties, ballet performances, and karate competitions. One couple was watching their nanny on a camera they'd had installed in the kitchen. She was making spaghetti. Where had all these children come from? They were climbing out of the digital woodworks at this party, and I was being obliged to smile at a ring of phones all displaying perfectly happy, mediocre children, and one nanny boiling pasta.

After I'd walked around enough, I found a few people who were still single after a breakup. Now they were reading self-help books and taking trips to southeast Asia, riding on motorcycles and working on volunteer boards, or doing CrossFit and hot yoga. We didn't have the time or money to travel. We were still stitched to our old lives.

Everyone seemed happy at the holiday party. Everyone seemed to have one or two dogs they loved and took on early-morning walks, and wasn't that the nicest time of day to be alone? The way the light had a tinge of green, and the sound of wet leaves underfoot. Wasn't the air so crisp at that hour? Some days when I wasn't working at my temp job, I slept until noon.

None of those people interested me. We didn't have a dog or children. My boyfriend was allergic to dogs, and I wasn't going to be anyone's mother. There were too many things to do in life—visit Argentina, learn to cook paella, watch the Oscar-nominated movies, practice meditation more diligently, follow up with my Congressman, call my grandmother—to be spending my time picking shit from the sidewalk or wiping a child's bottom. Mind you, I rarely used my time to do any of those things, but the thought of being unable to use my time as I pleased nearly paralyzed me.

One of the most profound features of my childhood was my mother's palpable loneliness, the way her face closed off when she wasn't talking to one of the three of us, her cheeks sagging, and her eyes looking into the distance. I didn't want to get married and have children and wind up feeling the same way, looking out a window at geese in a wild blue sky while children clamored for seconds on pancakes they hadn't helped to make, spilled syrup, whined about not watching cartoons.

In the distance, I could hear the strains of a Louis Armstrong song that made me want to throw up because everyone now knew it was about sexual assault. The group I was standing in had started a discussion of a Viognier. At our age, discussions of rubbery flavor in wines could last interminably, and soon people would be sharing about trips to southern Italy, southern France, other places I hadn't been. I excused myself and stepped out onto the porch, an old habit from when I'd been a smoker.

The eaves of the house were lined with long, murderous-appearing icicles. The voices inside were mercifully muffled along with the Armstrong. After a moment, I realized I was not alone on the porch. There was an older man, his elbows resting on the railing, smoking. We were on opposite sides of the porch, distant enough that we wouldn't have to talk, though it would be awkward if we didn't. Most times, finding myself in this sort of situation, I'd look at my phone and sigh, giving some indication that my presence had meaning. I liked to convey that people were waiting for me or I was in a hurry to be elsewhere. Anything but the reality of the situation, which was that I was rarely needed by anyone. I didn't look at my phone, though, because I remembered something interesting about the man. He had a dead wife.

The man's fingers were quite long. Once, years ago, he had played piano at one of these gatherings. It had been quite lovely, and his wife had stood at his side, her hand resting on his shoulder. And now she was dead, a car accident a few months ago. Was he thinking of her now, or of that distant night, the piano? Although maybe the two of them had been terrible and unhappy together. Who the hell knew anything about another relationship? I watched him, wondering what he made of the talk of fluffy dogs and adorable children. I wondered if he wanted to grab one of the icicles and go around stabbing people with it like I did.

I felt, standing in the cold and looking at him, a sense of loneliness—a loneliness I hadn't felt in years, not since my boyfriend and I had been together. I felt no one in the world knew or understood me, and perhaps I didn't know myself either, which made the whole endeavor of putting on a skirt and jacket, of leaving the house and smiling over glasses of wine and eating crackers and several varieties of cheese, seem pointless. No. None of us liked soft cheese. Is this what we were fucking living for? Discussions of brie? In the distance, cars were driving fast on a surface road, passing by like waves crashing on an imaginary ocean. The man didn't look at me, just smoked, holding the cigarette tenderly.

I used to write stories in graduate school, but I'd given writing up for a job in the admissions office at the college. Now I flew across the country imploring seventeen-year-olds to attend my small liberal arts school. Most days, I found I didn't miss stories at all. But now, cold and alone, I found myself reflective in a way I'd once found deep. In stories—and what are lives but stories?—you're supposed to talk to the sad man smoking in the dark. Maybe he'd tell me about an evening he and his wife spent in Cabo, or about their rituals, washing dishes or tending lovingly to a garden—snap peas, yellow carrots, a grapevine.

How are you, he asked, suddenly, looking at me.

Frigid, I answered. And a little bored.

Yes. These parties usually are, he answered. You keep waiting or hoping for someone to say something interesting. It rarely happens until too much wine has been drunk and then it tends to tip quickly over into sadness or gossip.

I nodded, thinking of his wife. The snow hung densely in the branches of an oak. The moon was soft, and I looked at the scaly, gray bark of the tree as if it carried meaning. I tended to look at the natural world as if it should mean something, and was often disappointed. The world was just the world, bees, butterflies, anthills, dust and dust.

Odd question, he started, but did you ever read Choose Your Own Adventure books as a kid? He asked this without turning to face me.

He had been musing, and I'd interrupted it.

Of course, I answered. They were all the rage. I had one about trying to solve a murder mystery that confounded me for a few months, and every page seemed to end in my death. It would be like, do you want to walk through the door to the cellar or to the attic, and both would wind up being wrong. I'd fall down the cellar stairs or from the rooftop due to some elaborate trap set by the killer. It was difficult to take as a child, failure after failure. I grew up in the eighties. Everyone said we were going to be a goddamn success. I was supposed to be an astronaut-senator by now.

There's time, he said. You'll get there. He threw his cigarette on the ground and stepped on it lightly. He said, I always hated Choose Your Own Adventure books, but I read them constantly. I hated them because they didn't have what I was used to, what I wanted. What I wanted was a story, a solid narrative arc, strands of a plot you could follow towards a meaningful conclusion.

I could feel the sadness emanating from him like the cold. And yet, it also stirred an intense desire for him in me, something almost maternal, wild. I wanted to hold him and for both of us to feel warm and safe. I wanted to drink hot chocolate with him and talk about our childhood. My thoughts seemed to be only distantly correlated with reality.

He kept looking into the dark. He said, I don't believe in narrative structures anymore. Death will do that to you. It will send you back to page thirty-two. I don't want to go back to page thirty-two. I was on page seventy-five.

I was silent at first, not knowing what to say. I want so many things. Some of them are probably silly. But I find myself just wanting,—I paused, aware that what I was saying was itself silly—I want something different than what I have. Better.

Doesn't everyone, he said.

What do you do to change it? This feeling?

We grew silent. I was complaining to a widower about my boring routines. I felt foolish. The night was colder now. Up the street, a porch light flicked off, and a dog barked quickly. I wanted to fix the silence that had grown between us, but my boyfriend opened the door.

It's so cold, he said. Come inside. I have wine. It's not terrible. It's rubbery, but I can't say how much.

I told the man to have a good evening and stepped back into the house, sensing, as I have on occasion, that I'd missed some iteration of life that should rightly have been mine. Inside, music was playing and everyone looked delighted to be there. People had wine-stained teeth and were laughing uproariously at a joke I'd just missed.

The next morning, at my job at a non-profit downtown, I mused on what the man had been saying about life. My life, not his. His life possessed a clear narrative structure he thought it didn't. He had a dead wife. It gave everything he did meaning, even something as simple as smoking a cigarette or going for a drive in a car they'd once shared. Everything he did was poignant, touched by her absence. I found myself greedy for stories for the first time in years. I wanted to collect his story and fold it like a note into my pocket and carry it around with me to the office, to holiday parties, to share with everyone I knew. Nothing had ever happened to me, and I suspected nothing ever would.

I wandered the streets at lunchtime—flocks of pigeons bobbing, women clicking along in heels, a man playing the guitar in a square full of sapling maples, their leaves reddened. I scrolled through my phone until I found his name on Facebook: Daniel Kent. In the picture, he still had a wife. He had his arms wrapped around her, and they were standing on a boardwalk, looking entirely normal, entirely alive. She was wearing a scarf and had a few flyaways. I added him and felt a sudden surge of happiness. I wandered away from downtown to a park with a grassy hillock and a small, man-made pond. A pair of geese were taking runs at the water, which looked like old, darkened glass, warped by time. I waited for them to rise into the stark blue sky. I waited and treasured my waiting, this feeling of something to come.

THAT SUMMER

That summer everyone was involved in a cause. Every street corner had someone holding a sign, telling you to be for or against something, sometimes both on the same corner. It was sweltering that summer. We stashed our freezer with popsicles and ate them on the stoop, while pigeons shat indiscriminately on the sidewalk. When we drove, we left pieces of skin on leather seats, browned our arms as we walked the sidewalks looking for a cause that suited us. We were young and cared about everything. We wanted to be in every protest, holding up signs, sweating through our shirts while we yelled at people to think just like we did. We were so passionate that we wanted to be on both sides, waving signs from across barriers at ourselves while chanting pithy slogans. We wanted to be a part of something larger, to shed our shells like crabs and slip into something new.

You wound up devoting yourself to poetry, and I wound up devoting myself to you. You'd lie awake at night reading Lorca, crying at certain passages, your nightgown half-open—collarbone exposed. I'd run my fingers through your hair as if it were silk, as if it were rain, as if it were a loom and my hands were thread, as if we would one day get old, as if we would one day be dead, as if we would not exist forever but only inside the eternity of this moment.

We told each other stories as we looked at the stars. You pointed out certain symmetries of night skies and the deaths of famous men. You said that Napoleon and Caesar both died under a full moon, that Mark Antony and Marcus Aurelius died when Neptune was at its brightest, while I listened in the cold, damp, evening. After you'd finished, it would be my turn to lie awake, watching the outline of your ribs, wreathed in skin, rising and falling—such a beautiful liar.

On the way home, while the moon lay like oil on water, I asked why all of our conversations were about dead people. You said you had more in common with them than the living, that they understood you were a kind of labyrinth, and life was a confused searcher. I kissed you on the lips, hard. I said I'd been searching for you all summer, through cups of coffee, trails of cigarette smoke, bits of glass upon the shore, broken fingernails and fingertips, the slight grazing of knees beneath the table. And you turned from me and said, "I'd like to get more coffee," as if the words were empty.

A week later I was gone, traveling back out West to finish college. I left on a warm summer evening—the sky purpling under a mass of cumulus clouds. After a few miles, I stopped thinking of you. I drove through the rice fields—insects pattered like rain against the windshield. By the time I reached San Jose, the dark hills rising like sentinels above the valley, I'd forgotten you.

Until tonight, when I was on the roof, stringing Christmas lights from the gutter with the children watching. I told them to throw up more lights, lost my balance, and fell. I broke my right arm on the sidewalk.

With that, you, and the memory of that summer returned to me. I realized as I lay there that I had not missed you in my mind or heart. I had carried you around in my bones. And now you had been released, the night was suffused with you. And as I lay on the cement, beneath a pinkish sky, with my family gathered around me, I thought of you. I thought of that summer, of all the summers that had passed since I'd seen you, and all the summers that would pass without you, enough summers to fill a lifetime.

WHEN WE LIVED BY THE SEA

Back then we lived within walking distance of the sea. At night, after dinner and a glass of cheap wine, we'd walk down the sand-dusted streets on our way to the water. The streets were serpentine and dark, and you could smell the sea as you walked down them, as if it were not you approaching the sea, but the sea approaching you. The cars along the way had rusted wheel wells and thin trails of salt on the windshield. At one time, we were deeply in love. The streets dead-ended, and you walked through a copse of eucalyptus, across the thin line of railroad tracks and down a dusty path, lined by iceberg plants. Beyond that was a sandstone cliff and a solitary dead tree keeping watch over the water. We'd often stand silently, watching the pale green water make its way to shore.

The top of the ocean is often placid, less like an ocean and more like an oil painting. Though some days the wind made small whitecaps on the water, splashing against the rocky outcroppings where seals sometimes lie midday. But even at its most active, the surface of the ocean bears very little resemblance to the riot of action below—the schools of fish, pods of dolphins, the crabs, seals, sea stars, anemones and on and on ad infinitum, because God didn't rest until the seventh day. On that day the horizon held a patch of low-lying clouds the color of tattered overalls, rimmed in pink. We were so lonely together.

Down by the green and blue water, three children were playing, filling buckets with water and sand, sometimes pouring the water over themselves, and at other times pouring it over the sandcastle. I said to her that children are strange sometimes, as we well know, working against their own good without seeming to realize it, blind or indifferent to the destruction they are inflicting on their creation. In the wind, my eyes blurred.

The children splashed water on one another as we watched. We watched because someone should watch them, down there by the water, with the light draining from the sky. We had eaten dinner, though dessert awaited, and we felt we could spare the time. The sea induced silence, and we welcomed it. We'd been fighting for months. After a while, to pass the time, we named the children. The oldest was a boy with red hair, and we called him David, which was the name of my older brother. He kept taking pails of water from the ocean and splashing the two smaller ones, surprising them, and their little backs arched and they laughed uproariously or started to cry and begged him to stop, such being the ways of children.

The middle child, though really we were basing it mostly on height, was a thin little girl, who had short, sandy-blond hair cropped at her neck. We call her Madeline after a character from a children's book that our daughter so loved. She was collecting shells of all sizes and affixing them to the exterior of the sandcastle, meticulously, slowly. She was careful and yet indignant and wild when the water splashed her. She reacted like a cat, her back arching, and sometimes Madeline chased her older brother, her fists balled as if she were going to squash him like an ant, but he danced away and back towards the water, and she returned to the shells, to the castle, to the work at hand.

The youngest was a small boy, barely more than a toddler, with sandy-brown hair that curled behind his ears. We called him Andrew, which was my name once when I was very young. The littlest boy put his foot in the moat created by the water, then watched his foot sink into the sand with intensity and delight. He walked towards the ocean, picked up a stick and experimentally swung it at the ground. A seagull flew overhead, passing on its strangely mournful cry. The bird and its cry, repeated as it is, time and again on every beach, should not have such a meaningful and lonely cry, but it does. Go listen to it right now. It might break you.

Soon enough the sky turned pink and gold. The clouds made a frame for the sun to perch in and the sea lay there, aimless, sparkling, and deepening in color, a faint kind of blue. We started talking to one another of the years that have passed, all the years that we've lived by the water and watched the sunset and the ocean without ever finding any meaning. Though it seems to both of us emblematic of beginning and endings, alphas and omegas—surely this water and light must mean something?

Down by the water, David had mostly tired of throwing water on the other children. He lay on his back, his small stomach rising and falling rapidly. The sun had almost entirely set. The water was now deep and blue-black. One of us thought they saw a dolphin fin, but we couldn't be sure. The little red-haired boy rose and walked out towards the water with his red bucket. His siblings were lying on towels, giggling at some joke that we could not hear from the cliffs above.

As the boy leaned down in the water of the Pacific, a wave knocked him down and carried him out. For a while, we watched his red bucket, tossed and passed along the shore. The bucket moved down the shore in the direction of the small current, away from us. We waited for the ocean to give back the boy, or for the boy to escape the ocean. Nothing happened, and soon it was pitch black. We sat in that dark, huddled together, waiting for what was to come.

THE NATURE OF TIME

I lived for a time in Spain, on one of those semesters abroad that turned into a year when I dropped out of school to pursue my dreams, those ineffable things that hang like mist over our lives. I was living then with a friend who denied the contiguous nature of time. Time, he claimed, was not linear but cyclical. Such that all things that had passed would come to pass again, Helen would launch the fleet of Troy with her face, Sophocles would sit down and pen the tales of Antigone and Oedipus Rex, and William Herschel would stay up for hours grinding lenses to peer at the stars.

"Meaning what?" I asked him, one day while we sipped wine and watched flies bump lazily into the windows.

"Namely," he said, that all the works of the world will one day return again.

Such a view naturally led him to support theories of the apocalypse, a second ice age and a new world born again from the old, but with similarities so striking as to be a facsimile of the first.

And so, according to him, we had already had this same conversation in Madrid in some different iteration of the same world, where we watched the city bake in mid-summer light and talked about the nature of reality. Such views also led him to doubt the history books, geologic records, and history itself, which he said were all designed to promote the lie that time was linear.

The great exception that we could come up with was the book of Ecclesiastes: *There is nothing new under the sun. There is nothing that can be said or done that has not been done before*. In this book, without a doubt the best in the Bible as a whole, was the trace of the knowledge that wound its way like a bit of silver light through the crack of a window, tracking the real shape of time.

By mid-semester, we were shirking off class to eat ham croquettes and sip coffee while discussing the nature of reality, which, to him, was an illusion. Sometimes we'd swim, and I'd feel a preternatural clarity beneath the water, stroke after stroke, which affirmed the linearity of time and causality of motion. I'd want to remain in the pool forever, affirming with each stroke that life had meaning.

According to Martin, linear time was the root of many evils. He thought that the doctrine of free will was contingent upon linear time, and that it led people to scurry about the world committing atrocities, believing that their time in the world was finite and that each individual moment was special and meaningful, when in fact, it had all already happened. This temporal idea, he said, was a central idea of the Renaissance and patently false. "We are but images and recreations projected across the landscape of history time and time again."

And though he was funny, often giving voice to the flies that buzzed around us and portraying great debates between the Sophists and Plato as though the flies themselves were the great orators, we were not able to spend much time in the company of other people because he was forever saying that he'd already had this particular conversation, of that he was almost certain, and so he was easily bored and quickly grew restless, often leaving the group to look out at a fountain or birds gathering in the street, and I felt compelled to follow. And so all discussion of politics, which were always in the air, or of soccer left no impression on him at all. He was concerned, only and always, with the nature of time, and therefore, with the return of Franco, the Inquisition, and Christ, who in returning would fulfill only a portion of his promise.

And though this made him an extremely difficult companion, he was also the most charming. For by denying time's linearity he also denied its effects upon him, which meant that he took incredible risks, challenging professors and public intellectuals, jumping from thirty-foot sea walls, approaching beautiful women at parties and asking them back to our shared room where he'd discuss time until he was bored. Since everything had already happened, he denied them as acts that had anything to do with him; rather, his actions were something distinct from him, and he was, in his mind, in the process of very carefully following footprints in the sand.

Eventually, the semester ended, both of us failing nearly every class but for one on the philosophy of Spinoza, who Martin respected, but who he also wished might return as slightly more like Voltaire in the next revolution of the Earth. We had tired of Madrid, and

Martin, whose father was extremely wealthy and well connected, agreed to send Martin and me to Italy. By then my parents were sending frantic emails to me and to the universidad, but I paid them no mind. Life occurs in moments, in fragments, and to return home would have been to assume a shape to life that I no longer believed in.

I cannot inhabit that period of time in my life without a certain nostalgia for the fog that lay on my brain. Though Martin said that everything had happened before, my experience was the exact opposite. For a brief time, I knew nothing of routine and familiar places and lived at the very edge of life, each morning, a cup of coffee or city square a surprise, a gift. To live that way, or so I think now, is perhaps the only way to live well.

We traveled to the hill country of Italy for our holiday. We stayed with an old friend of Martin's father, and this man, Pablo, owned a large vineyard that supplied much of the region's Chianti. The house was made of old brick and situated between the rolling hills—a kind of fantasy brought to life.

We stayed awake late the first two evenings, getting drunk with Pablo, who talked of nothing else but the vermin who were trying to eat his precious grapes. It was hard to move him on to any other topic. Everything reminded him of the grapes and the vermin trying to eat his grapes. We did not mind much as he supplied us with liberal amounts of alcohol and the evening often took on the shape of the wine, curling slightly at the edges, becoming hazy, such that his recollections and wild stabbings at imaginary vermin were the funniest things we had ever seen: this portly man, stabbing the air with tines of a fork as though he were a knight of the Round Table.

The third morning, we awoke in our small room, which faced east, to broad swaths of sunlight cloaking the grapevines that rolled away from us towards the next hill—a kind of wave of green and amber. The sky was dusted in faint clouds, and the brick walls were limned in gold. Such a morning should be enough to wake anyone up to the possibilities of life. And yet, as we sipped on Prosecco and gazed out over the hills, Martin's brow was furrowed and he sighed frequently. He said that he was unhappy, for he couldn't be sure if his memory of this particular place was colored by his previous rough visit, years before, or whether the memory he was having trouble displacing was a prior iteration of time, which he said sometimes happened to him. And he couldn't be sure if he was really here now, or whether he was remembering himself being here from a prior life. In either case, he said, it was time for us to go.

I couldn't argue with him much since his father's money was funding our trip. My parents had given up sending anything beyond pleas for me to return home and to rejoin the sensible life that I'd lived until that time. And so we went online and bought tickets for the train—a trip that would take us to the coast where we'd hike through small cities that hugged the ocean, which approximated infinitude with its capacity.

The air felt still, but the small stems of flowers trembled on the hillside as we walked up the dirt road. Martin seemed happy enough that morning, laughing and joking as he imitated the old winemaker, stabbing the air himself, waging a war that was without parallel in the history of the world.

"He's always been a bit foolish," my friend said, "which is one of his charms. In some ways, there is nothing more charming in a man than a lack of self-awareness."

Whether or not he intended me in this remark was unclear, but I didn't take it as such at the time. At the time, I was a bit in love with Martin. When we reached the station, Martin insisted that we stand at the edge of the platform, away from the crowds and where we could feel the whoosh of the trains before they'd come to a full stop.

The sky was like a cathedral, a row of clouds was blowing towards the green-capped hills, and it smelled of wildflowers and honeysuckle. Martin was smoking and using his cigarette to imitate the owner of the vineyard, stabbing the sky for the mice that haunted the owner's dreams. Nothing seemed amiss.

And then, as if he'd been preparing himself for it for ages, he stubbed out the cigarette, spun around and jumped across the tracks in front of a speeding train. His body was flung like a rag doll down onto the tracks, where he was slowly dragged before I could look away and could only hear the awful sound of the train's blaring horn.

The police arrived within an hour, and I was pointed out as the one who had accompanied Martin to the station. After it was established that I hadn't pushed him, I talked to the police of Martin, of his disposition, his thoughts and that particular day. None of the puzzle pieces fit together though beyond his understanding of time, which would mean nothing to the caribini, sweating in the warm afternoon sun, as we talked of my now-dead friend. For he was gone now and had achieved, in death, a final and complete silence of the thoughts that had driven him deeper and deeper into the spiraling catacombs of the human mind.

My parents were not well-off and it cost a great sum to fly me home from Tuscany, but they paid for it. I didn't get a job that summer, but I returned to school that next fall and after a few months I forgot most of the previous year. I got good grades, went out on long drives or to bars with my friends, thinking not of time, or Martin, but of the future, who I would date and marry, what would become of me in the uniform span of time allotted to us.

I live now with a wife and two children on the outskirts of Kansas City. On the weekends, I mow the lawn and admire the light sway of tulips in the garden, the way the blackberry vines turn towards the light. In my dreams, I often see him, floating across the blued space in front of the train, arms outstretched. In this image, I now see that it was he who was correct. For this dream and memory return to me again and again, such that I see

myself trapped forever in the thick web of time, unable
to escape that afternoon in Italy, as I am unable to escape
anything in life, the voice of my wife, the slow plod of an
uninspiring job, the grasping hands of my children. And
I see him instead, in that instant, embracing time, as I
waste it away on dreams.

A WOMAN'S LIFE:
AN ABRIDGED VERSION

Finally, they'd agreed; the house would be painted. They settled on a shade of yellow. She was happy about the color, and he was trending towards ambivalent.

They took breaks to make love while the child was sleeping. Afterward, she'd sit in the bedroom and watch the starlings drift from the trees like leaves in the fall.

Accidentally, she told her husband that she'd fallen in love with the man who was painting their house.

She did not know if it was really love or if she'd just missed having someone notice her. He told her that he loved the back of her calves, the spaces between her ribs. Also, he had a wondrous ass.

What would become of the child? A mother frets about these sorts of things. Sometimes, she'd lie in bed and fret over the child, patting the locks of his hair while she slept peacefully below. Also, she sits in the dark and frets.

Things were not going well between her and the painter. He was good in bed, but the main problem was that he wasn't all that bright. She'd say, "What do you think of

Hemingway or the Middle East?" and he'd say, "Not often." For a while it was funny. But being stupid wasn't the sort of thing that you could easily forgive.

Bees pollinate a swarm of purple flowers. A robin hops down on the lawn and pecks at the lawn. She has never felt a particular affinity with the birds. Her mother had told her that birds were dirty. It had the ring of truth.

They met at a cafe near their old house. The courtyard was shaded by a banyan tree of immense size. Their daughter was playing across the street on a pair of monkey bars. She was a dangerous girl. After a while, she said to her husband, "I'm sorry." He looked across the table at her and said, "I'm sorry, too," which was really just a polite way of saying fuck off. She did.

In time, her daughter started to grow up. She said things like, "I want to grow up to be an oceanographer, so I can help dolphins." Maybe I didn't ruin her, she thinks to herself as the two them swing on the porch together. They are both drinking from small glasses of lemonade and waiting for the evening to cool down. Mosquitoes are flying around in the grass. She can see them in the purple sunset light.

A couple of years later her old husband married someone new. The lady was a schoolteacher. She was short and seemed to be nice. She had large white teeth and smiled readily. *People are always getting married*, she thought to herself. *Why is this marriage making me so sad?*

One year she broke her foot while walking down the stairs after an ice storm. For a while, she felt shitty. She stayed indoors with her foot in a cast, and as she struggled to eat, drink, and go to the bathroom, she thought, *So this is why people stay together?*

For a while, her daughter wanted a tattoo, and she didn't want her daughter to have a tattoo. Eventually, her daughter got a picture of a rose and a vine, strung up the back of her calf. Her mother thought what a silly thing it had been to have cared about.

At her daughter's graduation she sits with her old husband and the new wife. They are all very cordial. She feels lonely. She spent a long time getting ready for the day, standing in front of the bathroom mirror and appraising herself as if she were going on a date. No matter what she did with her makeup and hair, the mirror kept telling her that she'd gotten old. She started to hate mirrors.

Her daughter did not become an oceanographer. She lived in San Francisco, in a small little place on Potrero Hill that overlooked the water. She was doing bookkeeping for a large company of one kind or another. She'd visited her daughter once and remembered feeling very cold.

~

When her daughter was fifteen, she'd asked about the man who broke up her parents' marriage. Her mother sat in a rocking chair that had been passed down through her family for generations. It was a really dependable piece of furniture. She was holding a blanket, rocking back and forth and looking at the floor. "Tell me," her daughter said. Her mother thought for a while and then said, "He was beautiful."

"Oh," her daughter said and left the room to cry.

Years passed as years do. Some years were better than others. In the interim, she got older.

"Everyone in here thinks I'm crazy," she said to her daughter, who was old now herself, as she was wheeled around the convalescent home. She was a little crazy. She sometimes made up stories about the squirrels on the lawn that were narratively inconsistent. Her old husband was dead now. The new wife lived in Florida and golfed year round. She signaled for her daughter to move closer to her. She had whiskers. "I am crazy," she said, "but I can't stand being here with everyone thinking it." Soon thereafter, she was asleep. Her head was tucked onto her right shoulder, and she drooled. An attendant wheeled her away and her daughter drove to the airport and then flew home.

~

He'd come up behind her in the kitchen, tracing his fingers along the back of her thigh. Afterward, he said, "Do you want to come out and check the work?" She did. She was the one who'd wanted to have the house painted after all. There were clouds overhead doing nothing. The work was a bit shoddy. In spaces, she could tell that the brick had only a thin coat of paint. He seemed proud of himself. Three years from now they'd have to redo the whole thing. She could already sense it.

A RETRACTION

After lunch of fontina cheese and fresh bread, taken beneath the silver leaves of olive trees overlooking the Forum, he and his wife wandered over to Palatine. Once there, they looked out at the small hillocks of grass, no more than a slight undulation in the land's straight journey. She was reading from the guidebook, and he was looking around at the crumbling facades, tumbled rocks and bleached stones. The wind stirred slightly, a faint effort.

After a while, they tagged along with a tour group that was being led through the ruins, each wearing a bright white lanyard. The couple was acutely aware of their lack of lanyards, but curious enough to disregard the feeling and stay on the tour. The guide was a handsome Italian man, with an attractive smile and a habit of putting his leg up on fence posts as he talked, looking athletically around. The guide said that they used to flood the stadiums and hold naval battles where the hills now lay, hurling cannonballs across the greened space while crowds roared their manic approval at the spectacle.

They learned a lot in the half-hour as a part of the tour group before leaving again to stare at the hills, two lost sheep wandering away from the flock. The husband felt something stirring in his soul. "Just imagine," he said, his eyes widening in wonder, "naval battles." The wife read studiously from the guidebook. She confessed that she couldn't see it at all. They just looked like hills to her. They fought briefly over whether the sight was interesting, her position being that it was, in theory, but not in practice. His was that he could practically see the men boarding one another's ships, the swords glittering in the warm Italian sun.

Years later, after the divorce, he acknowledged in an e-mail that it was kind of hard to imagine a naval battle taking place on those idyllic hills of Palatine. She wrote out a long reply but never hit send.

WINTER IN THE CITY

In the morning, light gathers in the folds of my comforter, while I think about how I'd like everything in my life to change. Life rarely changes from bed, though, so I get up to shower. In the shower, I sense something seismic brewing inside me, and I can tell I'll spend the whole day wishing I could tether the world to me, wishing that I said hi to everyone on the street or danced on the Metro. As the water cascades down, I close my eyes and say the serenity prayer. Deep down, I know that today will be like any other day.

To quell the seismic feeling, I lie in bed and watch Instagram stories. Someone is asking whether they should make apple or pecan pie, someone else has a picture of a bathing suit and is longing for summer, another person has stitched together several pictures of New York—the elongated shadows of buildings, a string of city lights, a freshly fallen snow coating a statue in Central Park. As I watch, I try to do so without feeling intensely jealous. I try desperately to not imagine their lives as my own. All morning, I cling to the thought that I am as real and important as anyone else.

Outside, row upon row of thick clouds have obscured the thin vestiges of morning light. The drive to work begins to chip away at my goodwill towards men. A large Ford truck cuts me off and another person jets ahead of me at a four-way stop. It is as though, even in my car, people don't see me. I think about honking my horn, good and loud, but I am aiming to be the change I want to see in the world. Everyone in this self-important city is listening to NPR, feeling terrible about the President. I flip on Christmas music and think of how I need to call my mother.

Once at work, I settle into my desk and do twenty minutes of emailing. My therapist has been imploring me to give dating a shot. I take a break from email and message every person I've matched on Tinder. Hi, I type. Then hi again. And again. I send my hi's out into the world one after another. I imagine the route my hi's are traveling through the city, flowing around the Washington Monument, switching lanes at DuPont Circle, transferring from the red line to green, riding all the way to Shady Grove, taking an Uber to a coffee shop in Shaw—a vast network of hi's linking me to every part of this goddamn lonely city.

What if no one is messaging on Tinder anymore? Should I have added Bumble, added Hinge, added all the other ways people try and find one another or get fucked these days? I walk past Jennifer's cube. She's reading a gossip article on TMZ. We chat for a while about our weekends. She says she's happy to be at work, getting a break from her husband and children. She says she's jealous of me for living alone. She asks how I feel about Meghan Markle. I say my feelings about Meghan Markle are mixed and excuse myself to use the restroom. My feelings about Meghan Markle are not mixed. I love her.

I walk to the meeting room at the back of the office. From there, I watch light snow begin to fall, the first of winter. Snow falls like sadness across the bare limbs of an oak, falls across the cement, coats the half-dome of an adjoining building, falls along the edges of a fence, coating the world in a quiet white.

I do five more minutes of work on a spreadsheet and contemplate answering a customer service email. I am unmoved by the contents of the email and possibly life. Instead, I daydream about the older man, David, I'd dated during my early twenties. He had been so emotionally unavailable that I couldn't wait to give myself to him. Or at least that's what my therapist said. At the time, I think I loved him as deeply as I've ever loved anything. I had wanted the two of us to sink to the bottom of the sea, where we could find a little cave and make love for as long as we both lived. We had been so incredibly happy.

I did a Google image search for his name, David Rogers, and looked at pictures of him and other people named David Rogers. The other David Rogerses were not particularly interesting. My David looked much older now. He had a widow's peak forming and his beard was suffused with white. There was a cute photo of him and his wife. They were wearing nice clothes—he, a black suit, and she, a backless black dress. His hand was wrapped around her waist, pulling her tightly to his body, and her lips were curling into a smile. Once, I'd hated her with an intense passion. Now the sight of her confirmed my daydreaming had been just that. Now was the happiest he had ever been.

With this knowledge of my insignificance, I felt I couldn't work anymore. I grabbed my coat and walked outside and into the cold. I curled my lips, mimicking David's wife's smile, and blew out fogs of breath, one after another. I am here. I am here. I found, in the small pockets of air, something comforting, and I followed that feeling to Starbucks.

Inside, they were playing Christmas music. The store was decorated with wreaths, snow globes, holiday candy. I ordered my drink and sat. No one waits absently anymore, so I checked for messages on my phone. I had a message from Andrew, who was forty-two. He liked old movies and skiing. *Hey, how are you?* his message said. Tom, who was thirty-nine, and who had nothing on his profile, had also messaged, *Hi to you as well, lovely lady.*

It sent a slight thrill through my body to read the words "lovely lady"—a thrill I loathed because I didn't want to depend on anyone else for my sense of well-being, but that I felt nonetheless. I wanted someone to say that to me every morning. And I wanted someone to say every dirty thing I'd ever imagined while we had sex. I wanted to go to someone else's house for Christmas. I wanted more than my small phone could contain, and I felt myself practically erupting for the second time that day.

How's the day? I typed to both, then curled my fingers around the warm cup, staring at my phone like everyone else. Michael Bublé was reminding us all that the weather outside was frightful. Michael Bublé was very helpful and charming, and I wished that he was messaging me instead.

Tom said, *I'm OK, but my day would be going better if you were here.*

Andrew said, *Not bad. How is your day going?*

With all the possibilities of language available to them, Andrew and Tom had said precisely the sort of thing everyone always said to me on dating apps, a pass or nothing interesting. My therapist said I had a tendency to rule people out without giving them a proper chance. And so, for once, with sadness accumulating outside, a half-inch now coating the streets, I looked back at my phone.

Is that so ;), I typed to Tom, hating myself.

Oh, not bad, I typed to Andrew. *The weather could be better, haha.*

I walked briskly back to the office. The wind was rising, shedding the last spare leaves from a row of gingko trees. It appeared as though small flocks of yellow birds were trying to escape the oncoming snow. The traffic was light, and the sounds were pleasingly muffled as they always are when it snows. I could imagine this small city street as a picture in a snow globe.

You bet. Just look at you.

Yeah. I don't mind the snow though. Did you grow up around here?

Back at the office, people were starting to mill around, talking about the weather. Evelyn stood by the copy machine, shaking her head and asking everyone who walked past when we'd be sent home. Our supervisors, seven men and one woman, sent out an email saying they'd keep us up to date on the situation, and we all grumbled to one another. I knew enough about the people I worked with, mostly women, to know home wouldn't be any easier. It would mean gathering the kids from school, getting them to settle down, do their homework, and keep them entertained all day with projects and coloring and Disney movies. It would mean sorting out logistics with husbands, arguing over who would shovel the steps and salt them. And yet, the idea of not being sent home left us all feeling frenzied. We had such little variation in our day-to-day lives. Couldn't they just give us the day off so we could feel, if briefly, on the way home, the small relief of change?

You're a flatterer. Aren't you?

I grew up out West. The longer I stay here, the less I mind the snow. The first bit of it is so damn pretty.

Anita said she was not having this shit; her kid's school had just called, and she had to go. It felt as though she'd won the lottery.

I'm more than a flatterer if you give me the chance.

Ah. Where did you grow up? I've always wanted to go out West, but I've never made it past Missouri. Which, just typing, reminded me how incredibly unexciting my life has been. But I guess that's precisely the sort of thing I shouldn't type. Whoops.

I could see the bosses meeting in the admin office. I was certain we'd be sent home soon. Those fuckers should have never had us come in, said Stephanie. If I spin out on the way home, I'm suing this place. I'll be on worker's comp for the rest of my life. I'll lie in bed and hate this place from an island I purchase with my severance. It felt nice to have somewhere to direct all the rage we felt at life, at the pettiness and insanity. Those fuckers, we all agreed.

Oh, yeah. What kind of a chance are you looking for?

I grew up in California. And now I miss it. The only place more provincial than New York is California, though. We're insufferable about it. As to your other comment, no. I always get really interested when a man says his life is basically boring. It makes me feel like I'll have a low bar to clear if we get involved. What else could a woman want?

Am I that hard to read?

I think you can figure it out. You're bright.

Ah. I've always wanted to go to California. It seems like a dream, oceans, and mountains. It's forgivable to be snobby about it. Phew. I was worried I had already killed my chances here and was going to have to go back to watching reruns of The Price Is Right.

On the drive home, the roads were nearly impassable. They hadn't been salted and my Civic fishtailed on a side street, narrowly missing a row of parked cars. Everyone else seemed to already be at home, their cars parked along the street, porticos of light flickering down the row of houses. I parked two blocks from the apartment and walked towards home. En route, I saw a flash of red inside a large tree. There was a brilliant cardinal perched on the branch of an elm. I lifted my phone, trying to capture the beautiful incongruity of the cardinal's red against the gray skies, against the white snowfall. But as I lifted my phone, the bird, for no reason, suddenly took flight, leaving a shower of snow as it flew into the wintry sky.

Am I? Thanks for the credit. Does it involve a game of checkers?

Oh. I wasn't asking to be forgiven. I was just saying it's one of my faults, my attachment to California. I figured you'd want to hear about some of my faults after you said your life roughly ends with Missouri. Does The Price Is Right have reruns, or did you DVR them? Please tell me you DVR'd them. Like most women, my dream is to date a man with a DVR full of old game shows.

I walked to the fridge and got yogurt. It was the kind of storm where everyone stocked up on food as though it was going to be apocalyptic. I had plans to eat yogurt and cereal for days.

Think a bit more bedroom, but the games part is right.

You have faults? OK. This is never going to work ☺. I didn't say my life ends at Missouri. I merely said the farthest I've been west is Missouri. I do plenty of interesting things like grocery shop and mark myself as interested in events on Facebook I later don't attend. Yeah. My DVR is full of 150 hours of Price Is Right reruns that I watch every evening. It's kind of amazing how much I know about the cost of detergents, new cars, and washers. Are you impressed? Please tell me you are impressed.

Several friends had cats, cats whose lives were elaborately documented on Instagram. I had been avoiding getting a cat for precisely this reason. I wanted my life to be about more than a cat. But as I stood in my apartment and looked out the window at the flares of streetlights, and the purple light of the snow, I realized life in this city was never going to feel right or fulfilling. And if I could only wrap my mind around that, perhaps I could carve out my vein of happiness.

I still needed to message my mother. I couldn't spend all night deciding who I wanted to be. I had to decide, at least for an evening, whether I wanted anything to change. It was dark now, and I was alone. I messaged with Tom for an hour. He kept begging to come over, but I messaged with him until we both got off in the dark.

Later, I sent a text to my mother, telling her I'd be home Christmas Eve. I waited for her to respond, but she must have been sleeping. I deleted all of my matches, then lay my phone down on the pillow and waited for the storm to end.

THE LANGUAGE OF GOD

I was twenty-three that summer in El Salvador, the first time life started to go awry, to tilt toward something beyond me, incomprehensible. I'd gone to Central America on a research grant to assist in a study on the development of the Lenca language in eastern El Salvador, interviewing the local population who were in the process of reinstituting their old Mesoamerican language in textbooks and schools. Our interviews were designed to serve as a record of their recovery, tracing the roots of this formerly fading linguistic identity. It was my job to record and transcribe the interviews for the professor leading the team—a rote task that suited me. The work was simultaneously boring and interesting, typical of academic life.

I was struggling that summer with meaning. I had begun to see the world as suffused with meaning, which made the confluence of meaning and meaninglessness in my task, important for the recovery of the language, but routine and boring as I transcribed, somehow satisfying.

The real reason I was in El Salvador was to recover from the engagement I'd broken off weeks before, a decision that had thrown my life into chaos. I couldn't quite say what led to the decision, whether I had decided we were ill-suited for one another or too young, but I had made the decision quickly and taken the internship in El Salvador within a week, leaving behind a coterie of angry aunts, uncles, cousins, who had bought tickets to fly out to a wedding that was no longer happening.

Everyone, including my usually supportive parents, were upset I'd waited so long to determine Camille and I weren't meant for each other. Of course, I wasn't sure Camille and I were wrong for one another; instead, I found the timing didn't suit me. I was twenty-three, an age at which, or so I explained to my father, the world shouldn't feel predetermined.

Son, you're better than this.

But I wasn't sure I was. As I saw it, life was underpinned with the assumption that everyone had precise reasons for behaving and making the choices they did. However, I was coming to realize it wasn't always true, that subterranean levels and thought processes existed, emotions I couldn't name, and these played a large part in the construction of my decision, and they were running wild during this period of time, causing me to wake in the middle of the night, almost in terror at the thought of my life to come. And though this terror at life to come often subsided by morning, vestiges of it still clung to me for the remains of the day.

Though I understood I'd unsettled the lives of family and friends and felt guilty, underneath that feeling, I discovered something strangely liberating. Until I'd made this decision, it felt as though my life was on a fixed path. Camille and I had met my junior year and had been planning our wedding since the summer after our senior year. Prior to that, I'd attended the same high school and college as both of my siblings, had taken the same professors for my general education courses and assumed the quiet life of marriage, academia, and children they'd chosen was precisely the same life I'd carve out for myself. What my family saw as a breakdown, I saw as an awakening.

I thought of Camille and me, how comfortable we were together, laughing on the couch as we binge-watched Netflix, eating ice cream from the carton, gossiping about our friends or sharing stories we'd come across on our daily scouring of the internet. She was, above all, intelligent, but though no life is predictable, I felt a certain panic at the rhythms and repetitions we'd already started on, like the way we'd briefly roll together, a moment's curving of our bodies into one another, before we went to our opposite side of the bed. What is any life but rhythms and repetitions, though? But the reality of that life began to terrify me, not because of any deficiency in Camille, but rather, because of my inability to create something meaningful from it. Like most people, Westerners, in particular, I wanted to believe my life had a destiny beyond something simple, beyond rhythm and routine. I didn't know if my desire was correct or not, whether I'd fetishized my Western individualistic attitude and made a monument to it or whether I'd made a decision that would save myself. That said, when I left for El Salvador, switching my phone into airplane mode for three months, I sensed

I'd gotten off the track I'd been on for what felt like my entire life. In short, I felt free.

Gerald, the program director, and I were staying at the Hotel Perkin Lenca, a long, flat wooden building with a large tiled porch, dotted with tables and wicker chairs facing outward towards the valley below. The hotel was situated along the rue de Lenca, a networked path designed to celebrate the tribes who hadn't been conquered by the Spaniards. In the evenings, Gerald and I would sit in two chairs while the sky went through various shades of deepening blue in the distance, shedding vestigial light on the rows of exotic flowers the hotel had planted on the terraces below.

Everyone in my graduate school classes regarded colonialism as anathema, and we'd talked about it ad nauseam in our international development courses, flaying the Spanish, the Portuguese, the English, the French, with our intellectual whips for their desire to conquer, to make the native people conform. Thus, the goal I was helping to foster, tracing the reinstitution of the Lenca language, could easily be construed as a liberal cause, freeing voices that had been marginalized or cast in a liminal space by the dark forces of imperialism. And yet, though I believed that critique to be true, at least on some level, I had a hard time justifying the utility of our actual work. The local population seemed to have made their own decision to keep the language alive, entirely separate from our interviews, which then took on an element of voyeurism typical of Western travel.

And the real rub was, perhaps our project was an extension of the very imperialist project we sought to combat. We operated under the assumption it was an inherent good, that our grant money and interviews would help with the restoration of the language. And yet, we also presumed our studies would lead to further grants and allocations of funds that would lead to more trips to El Salvador and perhaps a large-scale project including anthropological digs. In short, it wasn't clear if our project was really about the language or about the neverending pursuit of a legitimate cause for funding from our university, which, like pretty much all universities these days, was a conservative and monolithic corporation that needed to be convinced you were worth their money.

My closest compatriot was Gerald. Gerald was originally from Ohio, a family of steelworkers he'd been desperate to escape. He'd gotten a scholarship and gone out East in his twenties for college, worked his way through the perilous rungs of adjunct, to professional lecturer, and eventually, to full professor, with all the gymnastics of conferences and book chapters and manuscripts, blurbs and professional ass-kissing. The journey had taken a lot out of him. I sensed a part of him hated academia now, but he wouldn't come out and say it. He had devoted the better part of his life to it. It would be like disowning one's children.

Sometimes we'd talked in the evening on the elongated porch. He'd pause after I put questions to him, as though he were going to say something profound. But instead, he rarely said anything of note, choosing instead to look into the sky as though it held answers or saying things like, *That sounds difficult.* Or, *You make a good point.* Now I can see that he wasn't good with people, but, unlike some academics who are content in their narrow field, Gerald was aware of his shortcoming and it bothered him acutely, driving him further into silence.

In the morning, we'd go round the village, trying to track down various people who'd been involved in keeping the language alive. Gerald would ask politely if he could bring out his tape recorder, using Spanish. I had taken French and German during my undergrad and could only vaguely understand the conversations taking place. Though I didn't quite belong, I'd gotten the internship because I'd come highly recommended by a colleague of Gerald's, and the internship was a favor after the mess I'd made in my personal life. It was my job to record the conversations, some of which were conducted in Spanish and others which used parts of the Lenca language, and then to do my best to transcribe them using phonetic spellings.

After we were done for the day, I'd wander back to the hotel, through the sun-blasted streets. Often, as I walked, locals whom I'd talked to would wave to me. The people there were almost all uniformly kind; a trope of a Westerner visiting anywhere is to wax poetic on the kindness and joy of the people. I knew this elided the destruction of capitalism and imperialism, replacing it with an image of a people I didn't understand, ascribing feelings to them based on minuscule interactions that weren't representative of the whole. And yet, I couldn't help the feeling that indeed, people were kinder here, gentler. Something had been given up in the race for attainment that had structured my life like ties on a railroad until that point, job, marriage, achievements. Things that were perhaps not ends unto themselves but that had been pitched as such. Their lives had something uncluttered about them, a sense of deep identity that eluded me.

These days of recording and transcribing left me feeling exhausted and by the time evening came round and the air had begun to feel crisp again, when vestigial heat could be seen evaporating into the evening sky, I'd walk around town with my camera, waving to locals and taking pictures of people, rocking away in chairs, standing on stoops, going about the business of their daily lives. We know nothing of others' interior lives, or very little, and the snapshots don't reveal anything, but they brought me an intense comfort. Sometimes I'd be invited inside for an ensalada or horchata. Those evenings were my favorites of the trip when we'd talk in a scattering of language that would have made Babylonians happy, spitting in the eye of God, communicating mostly through the vehicle of laughter.

I thought this would be my life, recording during the day and walking the town in the evenings, running my camera along the contours of the city. Gerald and I never talked about the wedding or the sudden circumstances that had brought me to El Salvador. The hotel had a small front porch, with several rickety chairs, two bulbs, swamped by moths battering against the light, and we'd sit there in the late evening exchanging mild pleasantries in the dark. Perhaps this too was life.

It has been said by philosophers, ranging from the Greeks to Pascal, that the circle is the perfect shape, complete unto itself. If you want to conceive of the Divine, an elusive concept, picture a small boy blowing bubbles in the yard, wooden-slat fence, a little yapper at his feet. Now picture the small soap bubbles rising above the clothesline, passing beyond the tops of oaks until they are shapes floating against the ragged frame of the sky. In your mind, keep expanding that circle until it fills the sky, cirrus clouds, and atmosphere, until the circle wraps itself around the Earth, then a ring of planets, the gas giant of Saturn, Jupiter's moons, the Milky Way galaxy, then extend it out into the universe of darkness beyond, black holes, undiscovered planets, keep expanding. Now you are thinking of the circle, of God.

I wasn't thinking of God before the circles began. Rather, evenings I'd often think of Camille. She'd send me a long email, detailing the ways in which she still loved me and how she'd been spending her time.

Dear X,

These last few weeks have been some of the most difficult of my life. Perhaps the most difficult. When you left, though it sounds like too much, I felt as though a part of me, the best part of me, was leaving, too. Everyone here is angry with you. I suppose I'm angry with you, too. But what I find myself feeling most often is sadness. If this is actually the two of us parting, I should tell you these past few years have been the most rewarding of my life. I wouldn't trade the time we've spent together. The long conversations and laughter have become a rich part of the fabric of my life. See that there, rich fabric of life. I haven't lost my flair for the poetic.

Things here are much the same as when you left. I'm still toiling away at the office, managing a small staff of people who have roughly zero interest in following my organizational patterns but who must do so. In the evenings, I often cry. I don't say that to make you feel bad. Rather, it's the reality of the situation. Many other nights, I watch television shows you'd probably like and sometimes want to tell you about them but don't because you're not here.

Anyway, I hope none of this catches you off guard. I'm saying I'm still here, wishing you were, too.

It's hard to remember exactly, but I believe the first long and looping circle may have begun as soon as I shut the screen on my laptop. The email had left me feeling emotionally raw. I felt, as Camille had said, that part of me was now also missing, that I'd stored it away inside her and my trip had allowed me to temporarily forget its existence. And reading her words brought it all back to me, like an amnesiac patient, and I was swirling with emotions as a pile of leaves caught in a storm.

First, I stood on the porch, watching clouds painted purple by sunset, hovering like feathers in the sky. And then, or so I see it now, I felt compelled to begin walking and set out into the town. I see now my path that night was irregular, though. At the time, I assumed it was because I was distraught, not paying attention to the lanes, desiring to spend time by myself, taking a narrow path that stretched into the jungle beyond before eventually winding its way back into town. As I walked through the path, I wondered how I should respond to Camille, or whether I should respond to Camille. I either needed to end things decisively or reconsider our relationship entirely. Of course, I could also not respond at all but that would be a response in and of itself. My non-responsiveness could easily be interpreted as a continuation of the rupture, which meant I had to respond, either reinforcing our break or giving her the idea it might come to an end.

Birds were calling from the trees as I walked, various varieties I couldn't name, but whose bright colors of green and mottled brown flitted through the trees, creating an impressionist tableau of light, color, and movement. Soon, I reached another path, which arced back towards the town. I walked through an orchard of coffee trees—row upon row of evergreen turning a deeper green as the sunlight drained from the sky.

In town, I walked around in a trance, watching my feet treading along the road as if I were an explorer. I was thinking of Camille, and I imagined Camille was thinking of me. Though perhaps she wasn't. Suddenly, a voice called my name out from a house I'd passed, lifting me from my reverie. Daniel, a man somewhere in his late thirties or early forties, stood in the doorway of his house. Gerald and I had interviewed him two weeks prior. He'd given us the small bits of language he still exchanged with his wife, but he'd been unusually kind. He invited me in for tea, and I accepted.

The dining room was small and cozy. I sat on a couch, which I sank into, and he sat on a leather chair across from me. At first, I felt intensely awkward; a strange urgency to move coursed through me, but I held it at bay. After exchanging pleasantries about the weather, I asked after Daniel's family. He had three daughters and a son, all of whom lived within the city limits. Two of his daughters were married, a third at university, and his son worked at a restaurant in town. The son, he said, was trouble. He had always been that way, even as a little boy he'd always pushed limits the girls had not. He talked of his son, and I thought of my father, whom I hadn't spoken to in a month. For years, my father had been my confidant, but the breakup had caused a rift to grow between us, and I missed his tender listening and quiet advice. I had come to realize, now that we weren't talking, how much I'd relied on my father's wisdom and insight throughout my life. I missed him dearly.

Naturally, I could have taken Daniel's openness as a sign to share myself, but I was reticent, closed off in a world of my own suffering. I left without talking much about myself, touching instead on the details of the project, on our hopes of obtaining a grant at the state and federal level if the university stopped funding, of what good work we thought we could do to help the language continue to expand. I had no idea if I believed it myself, but I'd had it repeated so many times I passed it off as gospel. The truth is, I wanted to be home, or rather, a place like home but inhabited by different people who weren't all angry at me. Perhaps what I'm saying is I wanted to travel back in time and undo everything. Except, my decision had been the right one, but the aftermath had gone wrong.

That night, Gerald and I sat on the porch again, while the sound of insects in the forest battered the nighttime air. I found myself tempted to ask Gerald if he also understood the project as futile, yet another projection of American ideology grafted onto a people who didn't have much interest in it. But Gerald looked, standing there in the buttery light of the porch, so incredibly bereft that I kept things to myself and then slept.

The next day's interviews were canceled, which left me to construct my own afternoon. I started an email to Camille:

Dear Camille,

But that's as far as I got, or rather, I wound up deleting seven or eight iterations of the email. I sat back in my chair, trying to project my life forward with or without Camille, but the reality was that I couldn't even see beyond even the next few months, let alone a lifetime. I left the hotel and started walking again. I can see now that my walk resembled the walk of the previous day, almost entirely, but it wasn't something I recognized then.

You could reasonably charge any of the old prophets with religious mania, categorize them as bipolar. However, there is a difference, not subtle, between having a religion started after you or becoming a Catholic saint and our modern conception of religion. I had no history of mental health issues, and my religion had gone dormant during college, a relic as opposed to an active part of my life.

You see, these evening walks didn't cease. Rather, I found myself rather bored during the day, watching Gerald's quizzical face as he asked after the language, and the tepid responses he received. And so I started walking every evening, and eventually, even in the middle of the day, the world started to subtly shift around me, my thought patterns, for so long troubled, began to take on new shapes.

As I walked, I found myself no longer thinking of Camille or the sudden distance between my parents and me. Between the branches in the trees, I saw tiny blue patches of sky, and I understood how they'd been formed to weave together the fabric of the universe. I saw droplets of dew clinging to the edge of a spider's web, the tenebrous strands half-glistening in the last light of the day. And as my own thoughts began to fade, a faint whisper developed the edge of my consciousness.

At first, I dismissed it as some distant jungle noise, but over the course of a few nights, I began to realize the whisper was calling my name. And as I followed its faint sound, pulled along by the filament of voice, I circled the village again, the voice somehow growing stronger as I followed it from source to source, from beginning to end, out of the village and back in, the voice somehow everywhere and nowhere.

What do you say to people when you have discovered something unknown? What stories did that prig Columbus give when he "discovered" America? What wild nights must Darwin have had when he cracked the internal code of speciation? For, though at first the voice seemed obscure, no more revealed than the Lenca, soon I began to decipher things beyond my name. The voice was whispering about the dust of stars, and the woman who stood on the side of the street selling tortillas. It was telling me about a vineyard in Italy, and the way the sunlight lit the grapes in a green and peaceful valley, while at the same time recounting the day of a banker in Long Island, who was bored with his job and was watching the water while eating a sandwich. I could hear the plinking of nails as they fell to the street for a building project at a small town in Illinois.

It was as though the world had been cracked open for me and all the hopes and dreams were suddenly glimmering in the distance as stars in the night sky. As the circles tightened, the voice grew louder, and I started to see things from the past, like a middle-aged man bent at the waist, the hem of his pants covered in clay gently brushing the dirt around a fossil, his breath smelling slightly of gin, the hissing of the rain as it fell in a distant forest. And I understood I was now being given more. The sky was a kaleidoscope of colors, whirls of silver shot through with purple. It all made sense. Surely, what I was hearing was far more important than the Lenca language we'd come to study; I was learning the language of God.

As I searched for the voice, I sometimes missed appointments with Gerald, forgetting an afternoon meeting in favor of the walk. I came home, crickets keeping the air dense with noise, wondering how to explain to Gerald why I'd been absent that afternoon. Gerald was on the steps, looking pale and sad. Gerald, whom I'd wanted to replace the father figure I'd lost. Gerald, I said.

Yes, he answered looking back at me with red-rimmed eyes. But I found myself paralyzed, the words incapable of coming out. Gerald didn't know Camille or my life back home. How could I explain to him that my decision to leave behind the life I'd been building had been not only the correct one but a call from God?

Over the next few days, the voice grew stronger. On walks, I could hear the people in the village speaking to me through the walls of their houses. Colors were magnificent, multi-faceted, silvers and oranges I'd never seen, and I found myself able to understand the calls of spider monkeys, to hear the distant sound of rain forming in clouds overhead.

Women in the small town, who had once called out to greet me, began to whisper as I walked by. I found it impossible now to say yes when they invited me in for drinks, even during the unwavering heat of the afternoon. Thus, I formed insufficient excuses, eager to get back to my path. With this in mind, I began walking with my head down, avoiding the eyes of people I'd once greeted as friends, once drank beer within the late afternoons. I treated the world as a stranger, which maybe it always had been, and I'd been deluding myself until now, thinking I was a part of it.

To understand the infinite is to leave behind the temporal grind of day-to-day life. I was restless whenever I was with Gerald, only half-aware of our interviews. Afterward, I'd make some casual gesture toward recording the data and then set off walking. As the walks increased in frequency, they began to decrease in distance. I could hear the gas giants being formed in the distant reaches of our galaxy while simultaneously seeing the particular curve of a house along the river Thames, how pleasing the garden was when showered in light. I looked at the fingernail of moon and wondered when it too would make a perfect circle in the sky, an emblem of the living God.

Eventually, the circles became so small that I was merely circling the hotel, and the language of the infinite was humming all around me, like wires filled with electricity. I wrote to Camille.

Camille,

I am happier now than I have ever been. This trip has opened a space inside me, filled me with such radical things that I could not ever return to my old life. When I get back, I can share bits of this experience with you if you'd like. If I listen closely enough, I can see the shape of your life too as some other people might hear the distant sound of a train's horn. I have assurances here, things I can't talk about over email but I can't wait to share when I return.

I hit send and sat in the darkness, listening to the quiet singing of a spider in the corner of the room, who was weaving together webs of darkness and passing the time. It was a piercing song, with a tonal harmony that reminded me of sweet peaches I'd eaten in my grandmother's kitchen as a child and somehow also the way the basement of the house smelled in Pompeii, days before the eruption of Vesuvius. The moment overwhelmed me, and I lay awake all night, listening to the sounds of the universe, watching shapes play across the ceiling.

Eventually, the circles became so small that I remained in my room. I moved the bed and the dresser to upright positions, so I could walk in more perfect circles, my legs brushing the side of the dresser and my shoulders the bed as I narrowed the radius of my walks. It was hard for those two days, imagining what it might feel like to leave behind certain aspects of my life, my mother and father, my work, in order to learn the language of God, but I also was prepared to lose everything in that search.

It was as though I could feel God's hand on my shoulder, guiding me like a toy soldier around the outside of a clock. At the end of the circles, I was bathing in the light, seeing the face of God. And then it went dark.

I awoke with an IV in my arm, and when I glanced over, I saw a vase of purple flowers in the window, and there was my father, hunched over in quiet sleep. Beyond him was the world, but I saw something had changed again, and it was no longer singing to me. The grass was just the grass, the sky, just the sky. Camille must have called my parents after the email, or maybe it was Gerald. I suppose the fact I never left the room presented a problem that could no longer be ignored.

I sent Camille an email when I was fully recovered three days later, telling her when I would be home. I completed the rest of my stay in El Salvador without incident, eating, sleeping, transcribing. Father had wanted to take me home, but I assured him everything was fine, the mania, a new discovery, had passed. Eventually, I became again a part of the community, someone with whom the children would kick a soccer ball, and a man whom the men would feel comfortable drinking with.

Camille and I married at the courthouse a few months after my return, and we bought a house in the middle of the city with a small garden we could tend together. Years have passed since that fateful summer that almost changed my life, and it's been easy to attribute it to a minor shift in my brain chemistry, a temporary loading error.

Of late, though, when Camille and the children have drifted into a deep sleep, I find myself wandering around the house and into the attic, and I look outside the small window, through the bare branches of an oak at the moon held in the arms of the sky. And I feel something compelling me, something outside myself, to begin walking in a slow circle around the room, one foot after another, in search of the language I'd lost, in search of the face of God.

MOTHER'S GARDEN

After the call, I packed and took the first cheap flight home. When I arrived, mother was sitting in the kitchen, facing the garden—a modest rectangle of yard, at least for California, a yard where my siblings and I had taken turns toiling during our adolescence. In the heat of the northern-valley summer, we'd sweated while converting a boring stretch of grass and a single tree into a proper English garden. First, we'd pulled every blade of grass out by the roots, ripped knotty ropes of ivy from the ground, tendrils like a line of vertebrae. We'd formed mounds by slogging piles of earth around the side yard, then dug paths that snaked through them. We'd hefted brutishly heavy flagstones to line the footpaths, hauled gravel to fill the paths, dug a hole and lined it to make a pond, filled it with koi. We planted the mounds with primrose, azalea, blackberry, lilac, star lilies, rose bushes, and daisies. Welcome home, Andrew, mother said, reaching over her shoulder for my hand, then holding it there, as she always had.

I unpacked in my childhood room, bare white walls. As a teenager, I'd covered every square inch with sports memorabilia, box scores, Michael Jordan posters. A large shade now covered the window, where once the sun had blazed through on summer afternoons, turning the room into a sauna. The room was darker now. The changes discomfited me. It was as though I expected things here, mother, my room, to remain the same, while my own life hurtled onwards—marriages, children, divorce, career changes.

I lay on my childhood bed and looked at the ceiling, thinking of my own children, nine and eleven, back home, wondering if they'd fly across the country to see me too someday, even if their mother now hated me. I fell into sleep and dreamed I was a child with a fear of Dracula and the dark as I'd once been.

When I awoke, I was hot and confused. The world returned to me in bits. The bare white walls were the same walls I'd seen shadows on as a child. The bed was the same one I'd once lay naked on with my college girlfriend, our lithe bodies covered in a layer of sweat. I lay there for a moment and let the memories of the last few years wash over me—the leukemia, the things my father had said about me the year before he died. I thought about the slow accumulation of meaningless hours by a child's crib, my former wife's red-gold hair, which I had once adored. Thoughts passed through my head, one after another, as rain through sky.

Mother was still sitting in the kitchen, eating an early dinner. Your sister is arriving tomorrow, she said, a small bit of pasta attached to the balloon of her cheek. Good, Mother, I said.

Mother, I said, sitting at the circular wooden table that I had sat at as a child, what was the best moment of your life? An absurd question to ask an aging woman, but I had become absurd in middle-age, sentimental and confused about what my life was supposed to mean.

I waited while dust motes streamed in a buttery light, while a starling bent to clean its feathers in the boughs of the apricot, while a housefly battered the windowpane, while the television droned on with an ad about industrial glue, for my question had troubled Mother. Her downturned mouth pursed at the effort of producing the right answer. Mother, who had always given up self to her children. My phone rang, interrupting the moment. One of the children was calling, my son, to tell me about his soccer game.

In the next two days, my siblings arrived, efficient adults who had not been waylaid by middle age, but who had redoubled their efforts to structure the world around them, to bend it to their wills. If they could work out enough, set enough meetings and family vacations, perhaps they could control it, harness time. We talked about Mother as though she weren't there, as though she were a piece of property, something to be managed. They were not cold exactly, never that, but they didn't seem to see what I saw, flashes of soul, of something that made her a person beyond us even if she never claimed it, her right to not be Mother.

~

Andrew, she said, from her seat by the kitchen window. I have an answer for you. This is the best moment, being with all of you here, she said, seeing the people you've grown into. She smiled and took my hand. Outside, the rose bushes trembled in the wind. We'd buried our cat underneath them, years ago, a massive animal that had come when you called his name as if he were a dog. He'd dropped dead one summer morning with all of us home, as though he'd wanted to say goodbye to everyone first.

My brother was in the next room, gray-haired now and balding, tending to Mother's papers, and my sister was preparing dinner. In the yard, everything had gone to hell—piss-colored plants, nearly waist-high, grew on the garden paths, weeds threaded many of the mounds, beginning to choke off the flowers we'd planted over the years. The small patches of grass were returning, spreading seed and sending out tufts of roots, reclaiming lost territory.

That's lovely, Mother, I say. And it is. I'm reminded, as I stand at the table, of the Easter baskets she'd given us as children. She hadn't been well off after they split, but Mother would always get us extravagant baskets— chocolate bunnies, candies, yellow Peeps, jellybeans, round milk chocolates. In the morning, we'd rush to the table, to see what surprise was in store for us, to see what other wonders Mother would give to her children, no matter how much she too must have needed.

A SUBTLE PRISON

We were home for the summer, on breaks from colleges spread throughout the country, colleges located in stately cities full Victorians and craftsman-style houses and lined by colonnades of stone, cities wreathed in emerald-green water, adorned by public gardens, art exhibits, fair-trade coffee shops, colleges set in small mountain towns, where each morning the air was crisp and the smell was of wet leaves moldered in puddles, colleges where we'd driven up roads like threads of smoke and kissed girls in bars after we'd spent an hour discussing the ins and outs of Sartre and old girlfriends, colleges where we'd spent the year unlearning or playing up our rural accents as we emerged from the chrysalis of our small-town life into our new realities. During the year, we changed our politics and our identification with the things that we'd loved, sunsets over fields of rice, insects clicking in the distance. Now we cared about government work programs, about business, about what Foucault had to say about power and Hooks about class consciousness. We cared about anything that seemed ready and willing to shape the clay of self into something permanent.

Marc had enjoyed his college in a way that had eluded the rest of us. He hadn't tried to kiss anyone or assimilate into a particular branch of thinking that would narrowly define the prism through which he saw the world. But rather, he'd spent the year mostly alone, for his roommate was a partier who lived near home, and so he'd stared out his small upstairs window with lightly warped glass onto a courtyard dusted with light before turning back to his studies, which he loved with an intensity that none of us could match for anything else in our lives, not our love affairs nor our new class politics. He managed to love knowledge, its purity, its insane web of connections for itself, not as a means to an end. Marc had found a structure for his desires, professors who recommended Hume, Camus, and the works of Simone de Beauvoir, writers our small town hadn't guided any of us to. Marc relayed all this to us in a café, an almost dreamy look passing over his face as he talked about the way the streetlights flickered on one by one, the small pools of light he could watch form in the courtyard, and, in late November, the small snowflakes, the first he'd ever seen, falling in the dark. He was from a family of five and each day he found himself content to be so often alone.

Josh and Tommy attended the same school, in a college town where nearly everyone biked and waved hello and said friendly things. In the first days, they rode unsteadily, careening around the small roads and getting shouted at by other bikers, but by a few weeks in, they rode as though they were born to it, threading through the small bits of traffic. The two of them largely avoided each other, trying to shed their past as though it were snakeskin. But they both fell in love with an intensely intelligent girl from their French class, who didn't seem to know either of their names, though they'd both told it to her on a class visit to the museum where there was a brief exhibition on the works of Cezanne. She had a mind that was cat-quick, conjugating verbs and blasting past the rest of them, chatting with the professor after class. Her intelligence had a gravitational pull, and they wanted to be drawn into her orbit, to hear her talk again about impressionism, about the French Revolution or the sad sculptures of Camille Claudel.

Mike sat in hot classrooms, flies circling lazily, aimlessly, seemingly contemplative as he avoided listening to his older professors in excruciatingly long lectures. After class, he walked to the local coffee shop and debated the viability of the socialist state, about the need for open borders, and whether the internet was a tool for freedom or one more instantiation of oppression. Some days, he believed that the death of privacy would help usher in the way to socialism, a hollowing out of the old and pernicious idea of American individualism, replaced by an understanding that we were all a part of something larger than ourselves. He read Marx and Engels and found in those conversations the education the five of us could have never given him, limited as we were, by the past, which bound us to tell the same stories over and over.

Sean went to a business school in a city up north. He worked odd jobs as a waiter, smoking cigarettes in well-worn alleys, and cultivated the right way to shape his mouth when blowing smoke from a cigarette, learned to smile with just the eyes at older women across the bar, defended, with just the right amount of vigor, capitalism, and his choice to intern at a soulless bank, a large brick building that cast its shadow for blocks, to defend his desire to buy expensive drinks and pretend to have always been from that city; he laid claim to a new origin story, a story that put him in the heart of those cold cities, as though he was born beneath gabled roofs and wrought-iron fences, a child who had piggy banks where he had already started saving for the life to come, not because he needed to, but because it was fiscally sound.

I had gone to school in the mountains at a private college tucked between pine and fir, where the classrooms and dorms were the same building. No formal classes met at the school; instead, we had discussion groups that were conducted in small lecture halls that resembled log cabins. The teachers were mostly male, long-bearded with soft voices and wild eyes. They had us read Aquinas and Plato, the early church fathers. We had a weekend of silence where we were asked to contemplate the world through changed eyes on long walks through the conifers, jays hopping from branch to branch. On these walks, you'd sometimes see the professors, who had failed at life enough times to be content teaching at a small mountain school, breaking their own prohibition to talk with one another about Herodotus, Thales, and Cicero.

There were six of us home for summer, vaguely disappointed to find our town unchanged as though it reflected poorly on us as if we expected it to have undergone a similar transition, sent skyscrapers up and built a bustling farmer's market with fair-trade coffee. The disappointment could also have been with ourselves for not transcending our provincial town, for thinking that we belonged home one last summer with our parents, with our old friends. Within a week, it became clear that we should have grabbed unpaid internships, slept on friends' couches, done anything to remain away from home at our respective colleges.

We found our old rooms had been turned into sewing rooms, into offices, or into living memorials of the people we no longer were. We found our parents almost intolerable, constantly wanting to know what we'd learned, what we thought, what we wanted for breakfast or lunch, whether we were going with them to church. We knew our rebellion was nothing new, but we couldn't resist it; our newfound independence at school made assholes of us all, and we sulked in our rooms, on our long walks through the town with our mothers, saying almost nothing. We slept or pretended to sleep in the car, or looked dolefully out at the fields and glints of water.

We understood that we'd grown up in a provincial place and that we'd allowed ourselves to be defined by where we grew up, the ideas we encountered or that were foisted upon us. There was nothing unique about us, and this was at odds with the experience we felt building within us at college that we were capable of bursting forth, of creating a new world. That feeling seemed distant now as we sat in church pews listening to the pastor tell us about sin and redemption, about how all of us had been saved by a Jesus that we suddenly realized, or had always known, we didn't really believe in. We wondered if the last few months hadn't themselves been an illusion. What if our new lives were merely a sad reflection of our old? Though it had never quite seemed that way in classrooms or bars. Back home, we wondered if all our lives would merely be constructed for us by others.

The summer heat was intolerable and so were we. It hung in the branches of the jacaranda, whose last purple blooms were sometimes scattered by the wind. We knew we were insufferable, but we could do nothing to change our attitudes, our slumped postures, our feeling that there was something more to the world than we were presently being given. We talked amongst ourselves after church, in small groups, beneath the shade of trees. Birds flickered from branch to branch, landing briefly to pick at the ground. We talked in the coffee shop, in the back courtyard where a small fountain ran. We complained of our parents, our siblings, our diminished rooms. We complained of the girls in our small town, the way they lacked the razor-sharp wits of the girls we'd met in school or the well-ironed skirts. After weeks of this, we made plans to camp, to get away from the small town and just be amongst one another, as though we were a field of flowers all in bloom together.

It was too hot, we told our parents. We'd missed our friends and needed to reconnect. Our fathers, who had waited for our return, to patch the roof, the wall, to help check the garden or the attic, were disappointed in us, and our mothers, most of them, were forgiving. They saw that we suddenly found everything intolerable, and they wanted us back, and they thought this journey would help, and that somehow we'd return suddenly capable of helping with the dishes, of sharing our thoughts about the girls we'd met and the authors we'd read—our mothers, who had lived such provincial lives and who'd felt for years that they deserved more. They were desperate for us to grow, to validate the years they'd stayed, washed dishes and helped to send off college and scholarship applications for their best and brightest boys. And so they cornered our fathers and let them know that we'd be going, withstood the wrath, the shouts, implacable as stone until we were all free to do as we pleased.

We set off in the morning, leaving the paved roads after an hour or so and winding our way on dirt roads in search of the mountains. The mountains were dark in the distance, adorned with a row of cirrus, and we passed by fields of long grass, birds scattering into the sky, marshes where turtles sunned on rocks and herons bent languidly into the water. We talked for a while of the things we'd once loved, the nights we'd stayed awake playing games together, but then we moved onto our new environments, the lives we had so recently cultivated and left behind. Marc wanted to talk about something he'd read by Wittgenstein, but we soon found ourselves talking of the girls we'd chatted with, the ones we had secret crushes on, the ones with whom we were now sad best friends. We didn't understand ourselves in relation to them, and we often stayed awake late at night talking to those girls about other men who had disappointed them, loved them or not loved them, listening intently to their sadness and hoping that one day, as in a pop song, they'd realize what they'd been missing had always been in front of them.

After a while, we went silent. The sun was briefly shaded by a row of clouds like shale, then out again, bright and clear. We couldn't see anything of interest, just the red dirt road, winding towards the mountains, and a few stunted trees, gathering dust. We were silent for a myriad of reasons that we couldn't identify. Or rather, we had identified it but were uncomfortable. Here on the open road with our oldest friends, we'd finally hoped to be ourselves, the people we'd discovered in the back alleys, libraries and bookshops near our colleges, the people we couldn't be around our parents. And yet what we found was that even amongst our friends, we had habits that had calcified, certain jokes and manners of speech that had been among us so long that we didn't know any other way to behave. Of course, we talked of sex, like always; of course, we complained of our parents, but beneath us, like a fault line, we felt this new self trying to well up, only to be pushed back down by convention, by the past, by the heat in the back of the car that left our skin stuck to the seats, our brows covered in sweat. We slept or pretended to sleep as though we were in church. Our habits were as boring as the town we'd come from.

None of us had camped in this particular spot before. It was distant and obscure, a fact that made it appealing. The pastor of Marc's church had said it might take two days to reach. Our old high school teacher said that perhaps it took a day and a half, though he admitted it had been ten years since he'd gone to the mountain lake and that perhaps the roads had been improved, been smoothed and straightened by time, or perhaps they'd gone to hell, been overtaken by the surrounding fields and trees, failed at rivers or developed large sinkholes. In fact, he wasn't really sure, but he asked Tommy if he wanted to get drunk—he, who had tried to convince us of the genius of Rimbaud, of Keats, of Humbert Humbert, but whom we'd always known, deep down, was just like us, looking for a drink and someone to listen to him chatter about ideas late into the night.

We stopped midday, along a trickle of water attended by a willow, passing around sandwiches Sean's mother had made, sandwich after sandwich of ham and thin mustard that we'd stowed away and kept cold but that we'd failed to properly seal in the ice chest, such that they were soggy and almost inedible. We ate them anyway while Marc told us about some of the reading he'd done during the year of great philosophers. He told us that we humans misunderstood everything, and that the whole world and all its constituent parts were molded by language. Look, he said, pointing to the willow tree; we only think of that as a tree, roots, leaves, trunk and all because of language. It could just as easily be described as entirely separate things, such that a tree only means the trunk or the bark, or the root system. Language structures the way that we interpret the world. Whether or not he was right wasn't important. What was important, Sean decided, was that he needed to be drunk, so we got out beers, and we drank them and discussed whether Marc was right and whether we should think of the beer and the can as one entity as opposed to two, and after an hour of drinking, we were pleasantly buzzed, and the sky was doing absolutely nothing at all.

At some point, Josh and Tommy started discussing the girl in their French class, someone with whom they'd both fallen in love. It seemed innocent enough, but then they were wrestling on the ground and Josh was punching Tommy in the face, who eventually rolled back on top, spitting blood in Josh's face and calling him a bastard while we pulled them off one another. Afterward, they threw their arms around one another and laughed. On the ensuing car ride, they both agreed that the fight had been for the best that it had finally allowed them a release of the tension they'd felt those last two months in school, waiting and waiting to see if the girl would return their email or their phone call, wondering who she spent her Fridays with as if they were crazy people. The fight had helped clear their minds, and they left it both ready to forget her; such is the strangeness of certain moments in life, which seem to be one thing but are entirely another.

The road seemed to snake and bend toward the mountains forever. We felt as if we'd driven all day and gotten no closer. Soon, it was dark, and when we rolled down the windows we could hear the insects making a racket, rustling among the grass, burrowing into trees, taking flight from blades of grass, wrestling with the evening for control. It was Marc, finally, who made us stop. Originally we'd agreed that there were enough of us that we could drive through the night, but Marc, who was taking his shift in the passenger seat, awoke to the car wheels thumping along in the grass and careening off a small embankment as Tommy slept at the wheel. It took thirty minutes to roll the car back out into the road, and they all argued for a while, Mike pointing out that they were making good time, and Sean countering that it wasn't much use making good time if they were all dead, and all of us then waiting for Marc to weigh in with some dialectic about death from Marcus Aurelius, such that we agreed with Sean and started unrolling our tents from the back of the car, putting them on a flat space between the dark shapes of trees, on soft beds of old leaves.

We spent the night talking around a fire. It's amazing the capacity that fire has for truth. It awakens something primordial in us, and we all could see, though we weren't looking at one another beyond the brief second that it took to pass around a bottle of Tequila that we were shotgunning together, that what we had in common was boredom. We all knew that we had made the wrong choice. Sean knew that he was a fraud who belonged in the mountains, debating Descartes, not footing bills for nineteen-dollar Manhattans. I knew that I should be biking to class and falling in love with intensely intelligent French girls. And the two who had gone to a school with all bikes realized that they belonged in the city, getting in cars, driving beneath a string of lights. Perhaps Marc was content, reading as he often did, passing the time while the rest of us wasted it. Fundamentally, we didn't understand who we were, who we had been, and it felt as though life would oppress us in this way forever, asking us time and again for an answer we didn't have.

We awoke to birdsong and the gleaming back of a river, flowing through the countryside like blue glass. It was strange, or so we all thought, that we hadn't heard the river the night before, but we had all been tired, and it was dark. On our sketchy maps, we didn't seem to have any sign that the river ran through this part of the backcountry. And yet, there it was, clear as day.

Our eyes were reddened with poor sleep, but the slight wind and the slow rush of the river were too much to ignore. We'd wanted to get an early start, but we all felt the river pulling us towards it. It was moving rather slowly, glittering in the morning light. From up close, it was wide, wider than we thought possible given that we couldn't seem to find it on the map. Fish swam by in the shallows, and the shadows of trees wavered on its mirror.

"Shall we?" said Tommy, stripping his shirt off, and we all soon followed suit, save Marc, who reminded us that we were supposed to be on the road. The sun was still low as we stood at the edge of the water, stripped down to our underwear, already shivering at the thought of the cold water.

With a whoop, we all flung ourselves into the water, five arcs of water flying into the air. The water was immensely cold, and we felt every muscle and tendon in our body begin to seize. At first, our feet hit the silt, and we stood, pushing ourselves upstream through the current. As we ran, the water deepened, until we were all forced to swim. We'd set an ash in the distance, slightly upstream, as our destination. And as we battled the current something strange began to happen. Rather than inhabiting the moment, the piercing cold, the distance of the shore, I was filled with a lucid and intense memory of my childhood.

I was young, five maybe, wandering through the kitchen while a woman—Mother?—pounded pizza dough on the flour-whitened sink, working it with her strong fingers. The memory faded quickly, and I was suddenly seven and filled with quiet longing. In the distance, my father was leaving the house and as he bent to hug me, I saw that the man wasn't father at all. The person who had wrapped my body in his arms was a portrait of someone I knew, and with another shock, it came to me, it was a picture of my own middle-aged self. The ash was coming closer now as I pulled my arms through the water, still fighting the light current to stay upstream. Memories continued to flow through me as wine courses through a drunken body—a trip to Chicago to see a musical, the slow bend of the train behind a row of shadow-casting buildings, an evening spent lying on the oak floor while moonlight poured through the window, and I waited for my child to sleep. A portrait of myself in middle-age. I saw myself hundreds of places in those two minutes I swam, images so striking in their clarity that I felt I was experiencing my real life, while in a distant dream, I was swimming across the river.

When we emerged on the other side of the river, our bodies dripping water, a silence fell over us. Where normally we'd be giving one another slaps on the back and complaining of the cold, we stood in the buttery light, silent. Marc still stood on the other side of the river, fully clothed, watching us quizzically. There had always been something innately intelligent about Marc, something that went beyond book learning. His resistance to our absurd swim that day altered the course of his life.

For the next evening, as we sat at the base of the mountain, someone, Mike maybe, mentioned the river, and the strange thoughts he'd had as he swam across. In time, it became clear that all of us had experienced these flashes or premonitions as we swam. It was as though we had experienced a collective delusion, as though something in the water had leached into our skin. Marc had no flash, no premonitions of his future life. Soon enough, we decided that the combination of dehydration and lack of sleep had created a bizarre state that most people only achieve on drugs. We left the mountains after a couple of days, went home to our families and finished out our last summers at home.

It was Josh, months later, who first glimpsed the world that was coming for us. He was eating in the common room, vaguely watching each person as they passed, when he recognized someone, a young woman who passed his table. At first, he couldn't place her, but then, or so he said in an email to me, he remembered that he only knew her from the reverie he'd had that day in the river. As he sat at the table, contemplating how he could have already seen her, the young woman sat at his table and began reading a book he also loved, and he began to talk to her.

After lunch, as he biked along the wet roads, he remembered more and more about her. In the reverie, he had seen himself living out in the country—Montana, maybe? And he lived there with the woman he'd had lunch with despite the fact that he never truly loved her. In his most vivid memory, he was lying on top of his bed, his whole body aching with desire as she lay, curled in a comma on the opposite side of the bed, wanting desperately to pull her warm body into his, but knowing that to do so would be to extend the lie another day. He sent this in an email weeks after they'd been together. At first, he denied the possibility that he was seeing her in his memories and that his mind was somehow projecting himself into the future, but the more he got to know her, the more his memories of the future started to fill in the life they'd share together, the quiet fights, the long getaway weekends when they'd both drink red wine until they'd forgotten why they were angry, the orange sunrise pushing through the window. What to do with these memories? It was a question we'd all ask in the months and years that followed.

In the same town, Tommy had managed to become friends with the whip-smart young woman from his French class, and in doing so, he'd remembered seeing her in his reverie as well. In his mind, he began to experience bits and pieces of their future together, memories of his own apple-cheeked and round children exploring a pumpkin patch. As their friendship deepened, absurdly to him, for he never quite felt as intelligent or accomplished as her, he started to remember more of his life to come. He saw himself in a small apartment at the edge of a college town, living alone. He was watching a football game in a green chair and occasionally turning to stare out the large window into the distance at a parking lot and a row of sad pine.

For a week, he avoided his new girlfriend, with whom he was very much in love, unsure what all of it meant. But then, he made the decision that all of us seemed to make, seeing his life as a pattern expertly woven through a quilt. He apologized to her, and they went on a date to a drive-in movie where he told her that he was falling in love. Rather than dwelling on the inevitable end of their relationship, he found himself doubling the intensity of the pleasure he took in her company, her razor-sharp wit, and the way she sometimes laughed so loudly that he couldn't help but smile himself. It was as though his life with her was an extended summer camp, intensifying the pleasures because of the knowledge that it wouldn't last forever. He enjoyed their good years together, and even as they began to fall apart, even as she met someone new who interested her more in middle-age, he remained quietly content, knowing when to hold, and when to let go.

Sean had seen himself slowly rising up the rungs of the corporate ladder until he was named CFO, which meant that the endless piles of paperwork and corporate ass-kissing that might have driven him to start his own business were chalked up to small diversions on the way up a much larger mountain. He found himself working twice as hard to achieve a goal that he already knew was his to be had. And though he could sense, in his later years, that he would ask, time and again, if the work and toil had been worth it, still, he continued on. Because he knew he could quiet those questions by remembering himself at nineteen, someone who dreamed of driving fancy cars and drinking expensive French wine. He had made it, whether he believed it later in life or not. The emptiness, or so he saw it, as we all talked through the years, was just a part of life, no different than having hair or ears.

Mike grew into a father of three children, a destiny that he hadn't seen for himself, pulled along as he always had been by those around him. He always understood that he would acquiesce to what someone else wanted from his life, would mold and shape himself to whomever he was around. Thus, though he hadn't seen himself with children, he took to the idea, knowing that he'd become at least a passable father because he would learn to shape himself to his children, would achieve, if not happiness, a sort of contentment that this was how life should be led. In a way, his passivity made the transition into the future the easiest of any of us. The current of that river pulled him through the rest of his life.

Marc, of course, never stepped into the river. He waited on the shores for us to swim back, quietly reading a book. He looked at us as we swam ashore, lightly astonished. It was as though, without even knowing, that he sensed something in us had changed.

Did we envy his lack of knowledge?

For, rather than resisting our futures, we found ourselves desiring them, scratching off each milestone we'd already reached in our minds, curious to see when it would happen in our lives. There wasn't something inescapable about our memories, no desire to reshape our lives, but rather it was as though we had a guide gently pulling us across the river of life. Who were we to try and disturb it?

Marc disappeared a few years later on a flight to Thailand in a small plane from Cambodia. Strangely, we all knew that something would happen, but not what, exactly—a falling out, a sudden death—because our future memories never carried a trace of him. In a way, when his flight went down, I felt I'd lost the last connection to whoever I was before I swam upstream in the river of time.

Every year, though, as many of us as can make it drive through the countryside toward the mountain. The roads aren't all dirt now, and they have been made clearer. And we drive that lonely road, catching up with one another and looking for the river that appeared that day. Are we in search of our former lives? What middle-aged person isn't in search of youth now gone?

We found ourselves, living more and more in the future, frittering away the days at the office on email, on checking various gossip and sports websites. Rather than inhabiting our lives, we were eager for that next landmark, that next confirmed memory, which would let us know that we were still on the right path. We found ourselves terrified if we thought we'd missed something, somehow gotten to be forty-five without having that sad little going-away party we had seen. But no, it happened the next year, when we were forty-six. Everything was OK.

As for me, for years, I swam across every river I could find, hoping for something magical to happen again. I was different than the rest, I suppose; even in knowing my future, I yearned for myself back on the shore, with life still unfolding as a mystery. Though I saw how the people around me struggled with the weight of that mystery, wondered deep into the night about this or that lover, whether they should leave their job, have a third child, or move to a new city. Each decision was fraught, exhausting. And though we all had long stretches of life we hadn't remembered yet, still, in the distance, like a lighthouse, were some markers, a wedding we attended, a family trip to the coast, something that kept us rooted, confident.

But for some reason I found myself, unlike the others, wishing for something else, a different path for my life, which was, by all external measures, happy and good. It was this quiet yearning for some new vein of life to mine that had me awake in the morning often, listening to the birds chatter in the darkness. I was absurd, and I knew it. I had been given a gift, that of divine foreknowledge, and yet, it still wasn't enough. What I wanted was to know everything or nothing. The scraps that I could gather, the things I lived toward, were never fulfilling enough.

Sometimes in my dreams, I stand on the shore of a river, threading through the countryside like a snake with a glittering back. And beyond that river are a thousand more rivers. And as I start to shed my clothes, my mind awakes, subtly, and I see that these are no longer my dreams, but the dreams of a much older man, clinging to the last vestiges of life. Am I dreaming of my own death? At the shoreline, I fight and fight to stay ashore, but my future self, my real self, calmly slips into the water and swims through one river and then the next. Overhead, the clouds are pinwheels, low and pink. I can feel my future self swimming through the rivers in search of the past, in search of me, still middle-aged, wishing that he still had the power to change everything, anything. Even as I sleep, I feel the subtle prison of this, my second life.

THE SPACE BETWEEN US

Shana and I are in Italy: twenty-eight, unmarried, drinking and sad, still young enough to believe people should stay in love. We're at a party in the San Vitale Quarter of Bologna with newly minted friends, the sort you make when you are traveling, saving money on food and spending it on alcohol. Our new friends are good-looking blonds from some Nordic country we'd never visit. If we've learned anything in our eight years together, it's that we both hate the cold.

I'm standing against a gray wall beneath a print of Reuben's *Samson and Delilah* and watching the nylon-covered legs of women pass through the artificial light of the patio. I am in a sea of unfamiliar faces, and everyone is speaking a language I don't understand. It feels as though I have returned from space to find the whole world changed.

Shana and I pass the time with sweating drinks in our hands, reminiscing about our first night in Bologna. That night, under the influence of gin, we'd wandered dim streets with broken cobbles, past fading pastel houses, black grates on windowsills, mauve pottery that held bouquets of flowers. It was cold; the cement smelled like winter. We walked down Via Independenza beneath the porches that lined the main street—stores offering harbors of light. We entered a large town square of red brick, walled off on our right by a castle, crenellations intact. I thought of telling her about Henry the VIII, how he'd killed all his wives because they wouldn't bear him sons, and how we know now that it is the man's responsibility to father sons and how sad it was that so many English women lost their heads.

A statue of Neptune stood in the center of the square, bravely nude, cobwebbed in a feathery yellow by lamps hanging from brick walls. Four statues of mermaids flanked Neptune, water shooting from their nipples. We sat on a rectangular bench encircling the statue as stars appeared.

"Do you remember how we both wanted to be astronauts?" she said, turning to face me, the light caught in her eyes, a stray hair caressing her cheek.

"How could I forget?" I said, turning away from her and towards the stars.

"We talked about it on our first date," she said, and I could hear it in her voice, the yearning to have me turn toward her.

"Now that, I have forgotten," I said, not wanting to talk anymore, content just to be there, the same way we'd been in our third-grade classrooms, a thousand miles apart, but still beneath the same light of the sun, watching *Challenger* take off from Merritt Island.

"I still think my version is right," she said.

"When have you ever thought you were wrong?"

I swore that I remembered *Challenger* leaving the Earth's atmosphere, a meteor that parted the clouds like the prow of a boat through water. She remembered it falling faster, barely reaching the blue of the sky before arcing down towards the sea. It was in the air for seventy-three seconds, our brief dream. They say that the crew disintegrated over the ocean, or died from the impact. Both of us remember that day the same, though—the quick-shifting of childish dreams in the aftermath of the explosion. We were not meant to leave this Earth.

"There's the Great Bear," I said. Then, I moved my hand across the blackness at the speed of light and pointed to a new spot. "There's the Little Bear." Shana rested her head on my thin shoulder and closed her eyes. We remembered that first night as our best because that's the way of things; they always feel good at first.

The night she told me she was pregnant—seven months ago—I drove up the dim road into the brown foothills behind our apartment complex. I parked and walked through a field of dry grass, burs sticking to my jeans, to a black pool of water reflecting stars. I thought of my childhood, the days with my mother in church, of God, promising Abraham descendants as numerous as the stars. I dipped my toe in the water. The stars wavered and faded as little waves broke on the loam, and I thought that if I could make all the descendants of Abraham disappear with my toe, then maybe we could make it work.

We'd spent two weeks walking the cobblestone streets of Bologna—naked statues pissing eternal rivers, bars with circular tables, and restaurants, where old men scribble bills on tablecloths to avoid taxes. We'd walked through the open-air market where fresh rabbits hung, folds of pink skin and white muscle, only the eyes remaining, staring at nothing.

"That's so sad," Shana said, pointing to the rabbits. She told me about the pet rabbit—Chocolate Charlie— she'd had as a child. They'd loved him when he was new, when he fit in the palm of their hands, his breath, a feather on their fingers.

"But he got old, less cute. He sat in the corner of his wire cage on a pile of shit like it was treasure until the day he died."

"Is that something I should be worried about?"

"What?"

"You locking me in a cage with a pile of my own excrement when I'm no longer cute."

"Oh, honey, the word is shit," she said, smiling, but with a distant look in her eyes. "You know, his funeral was the first of my life. I remember my mother telling me that he'd passed into some other place. I believed her."

"Childhood is about believing in things, though, isn't it?" I said.

Italian socialists are smoking cigarettes on the balcony in the rain. A striking dark-haired girl with a perfectly curved ass is barefoot and swinging her toes through small puddles. She holds a cigarette between her middle

and index fingers, ashing on the tiles. It's as beautiful—
her gesture, the thin white fingers tapping the railing—
as all the pollution-inspired violet sunsets I've seen drop
below the hills behind our complex.

"What are you staring at?" Shana asks.

"Nothing," I say. "It's just strange to be in a place
where you don't understand a damn word that's being
said."

"Sounds like heaven," she says, and her eyes go blank
as she pulls absently at a stray hair.

I feel like we are astronauts traveling through the
vacuum of space, and I want to tell her everything, but I
can't take off my helmet, or I'll suffocate.

"I'm suffocating," I say.

"No sex games tonight," she answers.

We haven't been talking since the morning of the
miscarriage. That day, I came back from the park and
lay on the couch in front of the television, pretending to
sleep. She didn't ask me where I'd been; she took apart
the crib in the dark.

As I lay there, listening to her, blue light poured out
of the television through a satellite a million miles away.
I thought what a miracle it was that we could speak
to each other from across the galaxy, but how sad and
strange it is that the words mean nothing.

The next morning, I dug through the trash and
found every part of the crib. For the first time in my
life, I worked on putting something together. I worked
like a man is supposed to, on something that could be

completed. I committed my whole day to restoring the crib while Shana slept in the bedroom with the shade closed.

She came downstairs once and shook her head at the mess on the floor. "What the hell are you doing?" she asked, eyes, red-rimmed.

"I'm working," I said, putting the screwdriver carefully back into the case, the way my father used to.

She sighed, and went into the kitchen, opened the cupboard, took crackers into bed.

I finished putting the crib together. As I tightened the last screw and stood to behold my work, I was filled with a strong feeling of satisfaction. I had shown my son how to build something. I walked into the back yard and sat in the lone chair. A stray cat walked along the fence line, tail-twitching to keep balance. The light drained from the sky. I looked at our cherry tree, green buds showing months too early to avoid frost.

In the morning, Shana and I are hiding from the sun in a boxy room on Via Romita. We're renting it out on the cheap from an Italian babushka or whatever. The curtains are closed, and we're lying in the dark on an old stained mattress as roaches scuttle across the floor. It smells of old semen and burnt hair. I trace the sharp angle of her hip bone, where it rises, like a dorsal fin, from beneath layers of skin.

I've got a headache; my tongue is thick in my mouth, and I'm daydreaming of water. Shana's stomach rises and falls in the half-lit room. Her tits are spread apart and flat. I lap water from the faucet like a dog. On the way back to bed, I put a cigarette out on a roach's back. He lies there, and I wonder if he is in the space between life and death, between the stars, then scurries toward the wall. "What noise is this? Not dead? I that am cruel am yet merciful," I say, trying to put heel to roach.

"No fucking Shakespeare when I'm hungover," Shana says.

I lift my foot and brush the half-broken body beneath the sink. "You look horrible," she says.

I throw a pillow at her. "Your nudity offends my Puritanical proclivities," I say, facing the water-stained wall. "Let me know when you're all tarted up so I can speak to you properly."

"Did Shakespeare ever use the word 'tart'?"

"Prodigiously."

Shana throws her underwear into my back. "It strikes where it doth love."

I climb into bed, and Shana rolls to face me. A line appears on her forehead, and I become scared of what she might say, so I start naming the roaches scurrying across our frail lit floors, throwing my shoe at them, extinguishing them early, like light on a winter's day.

"We can't use the same name twice," Shana says, slipping on her shirt.

"That one's Magellan," I say. "He's circumnavigating the room."

~

By the end of an hour, we're calling them He That Rides the Pale Horse at Noon or Shitonya, names we'd heard on television talk shows or read in history books when we were less afraid of ourselves.

We eat at a bar on the corner of Via Independenza beneath terra-cotta arches with peeling paint. A sudden rain falls in the street. We let time pass. Long-haired men ride by on mopeds over wet stones, and underfed Italian waifs clop by on expensive heels. A pigeon hops by, a piece of garbage held in his beak like a prize. Above him, his brethren shit on a fading mural.

"Where are we going?" Shana asks, stirring the coffee with her finger. "Maybe we should climb the Torre degli Asinelli today," Shana says. "It's one of the tallest towers in Italy."

"I didn't realize I was traveling with an official guide. Somebody boned up on their *Jeopardy!* before leaving California."

"Alex Trebek is a sex God," she said.

"Those Canadian men: always fucking our best and brightest."

"Can you think of any other Canadians?"

"Not offhand, but I'm certain they exist."

I tell her that I've been dreaming of water and that we're being called to Venice. We take the bus down Via Independenza, passing exposed brickwork and expensive stores on the way to the station. The sky is cigarette ash, and neither one of us believes in dreams, God, or each other.

We board the train and sit in a car by ourselves. Beyond the window, businessmen read the newspaper and smoke. Trash blows from concrete onto the tracks.

"Italy would be great if it weren't for all the dirty Italians," I say.

The train idles, and Shana sleeps. Beautiful, long-legged foreign women board trains to places I've never been, and I think of leaving Shana—sleeping on the train—and following them to a distant place, where we could make the indescribable love of people who know nothing but each other's body. I imagine Shana sleeping as the train passes through the countryside until a dark Italian man puts his finger on her lips. When she wakes, they will talk for hours, and he will find all the beautiful things inside her that I'd lost.

Shana wakes and smiles at me in the innocent way of a child freshly returned from the world of dreams. The train hums and moves out of the station. Green hills appear, and rivers running through tall grass. We pass through tiny hamlets where houses dust the hillsides like snow. I get up to pee but walk slowly past the other cars: two men sleep, arms touching, with backpacks on; a bored woman stares out the window at cows and vineyards; a father, gray hair at his temples, reads to his son. All this domesticity comes to me through a barrier of glass, thick as a hospital window, where fathers dream lives for sons. I go back to Shana and watch her sleep, and I want to wake her, but she is as far away as those childhood dreams of reaching the moon.

We don't speak for miles of rails. I read out of a guidebook, and she drools on the window. The harbor of Venice appears lined by the skeletal outlines of ships; the gray sky spits rain. I run my finger across the ghostly veins on Shana's hand; sunlight appears on the prow of a schooner.

"If we are in space, we have finally found the sun," I say.

She smiles at me again, her face suddenly light, as though the shadows have passed.

The brick walls of the Santa Lucia station are covered in graffiti. Outside, the clouds have lifted to reveal an unimaginably vaulted sky. We stand in the sudden light, on wet stone steps, looking over concrete to the Grand Canal. The boats move through the water and part green water like silk. Exhaust pours from their tailpipes and fades like ashes into water. I shield the sun from my forehead with my palm. "Mine eyes have seen the glory," I say.

"No politics," she says, and pulls a laminated map from her backpack and asks what I'd like to see.

"I'd really like to see some more men's penises," I say.

"I don't think they have a lot of sculptures here. Besides, that's all you ever want to see; pick something new."

"I've got nothing," I say. "I came to Italy for the express purpose of withered penises and have been sorely disappointed thus far."

We buy tickets and board the number one vaporetto. We push through the mob of people armed with digital cameras to get the best view of the drowning city. And I wonder what makes any of us here feel unique, staring at the same few things, but maybe that's the point, that we're all sharing it together, like all the stars of Abraham casting distant light that still falls on this same planet.

Mansions line the water, hemming in the gondolas, vaporettos, and water taxis, like ancient guards of some long-dead city. We coast over the green water beneath a ribbon of blue sky. The palaces have bricked-up bottom floors and moss-lined steps. The water rises on all sides, staining the siding. Buildings are veiled in thick curtains, too blackened by the exhaust of passing boats. We float past fading Byzantine structures whose windows are lined with crosses. We coast past thick gothic structures with porticos for street vendors to hawk fresh vegetables. Everywhere, brick is turning to chalk.

"How did they build this?" a fat guy keeps asking his bored kids.

"By hand," one of them says.

The wind is rushing in our faces, and Shana is standing at the railing, a hand keeping her hair in place.

"Can you believe that little bastard?" I asked.

"I didn't realize your powers of deduction were so shrewd, Dear Watson."

"Oh, yeah, there's no way that handsome little devil came from him."

"Postman?"

"I was going to go with gardener, but I'll accept postman."

A woman, with short dark hair and thin glasses, reads to her children from a guidebook. She points to the Ca' d'Oro, noting that the brilliant façade still remains; water laps at the porticos lining the bottom floor. The children look on with mild interest, shading their eyes from the sun. Her husband's hand is wrapped tightly around a stroller.

We pass underneath the brilliant Via Rialto—the first bridge in Venice—lined with people taking pictures of other people.

Shana leans on the white railing, listening to the speech as the wind stirs her hair. The woman describes the baroque architecture exemplified by the massive octagonal crown-shaped Santa Maria della Salute, which is made of white brick and two massive double domes with a statue of the Virgin ruling over the sea. I notice that as the woman has been reading she's forgotten her purse, which rests between my feet. I lift her purse from the ground and move to the center of the boat. I stand in the same sea of unfamiliar faces, happy to blend in, waiting to disembark at St. Mark's Square.

Shana slips to my side, and we drift off into the current of people. We hear a commotion coming from the boat. A woman has lost her purse. I pull Shana's hand to my chest; I want her to feel it beating furiously. She pulls her hand away, unsure of the gesture.

We walk out of the main square as light begins to settle on the water. We turn onto narrow, winding streets with worn-away facades, pass houses, brown shutters open to the alley.

"Do you think brown is my color," I ask her, turning a leg in what I think is a girlish manner.

"No, and where the hell is this city park supposed to be?"

"Because I really like how it matches my shoes," I say.

She turns, and her eyes are bright, alive. "What the hell are you doing with a purse?"

"Accessorizing." And there is a strange difference between what I mean to say and what I've done.

"What is wrong with you?" she asks.

I think of asking her the same thing, but silence is best. When we reach the park, Shana sits on a redwood bench beneath a canopy of dying trees.

"Are we criminals now?" she asks. "Is that what we're going to do? Go around stealing from the rich and giving to ourselves?"

Her lips are shaking, and a strand of hair has broken free and is bisecting her face.

"I found it on the ground," I say. I feel a surge of feeling towards her; I want to brush the stray hair from her face and wrap my arms around her. I want to touch her.

"If we were in Pakistan, do you realize that's what they'd to you?" she says, gesturing to the statue of an armless woman across from us.

"Turn me into a woman?" I answer.

"This is serious," she says. "This is not some fucking childish game."

"Are you going to turn me in?"

"I should," she answers, and we sit in the cold. An elderly man tosses flakes of white bread into a flock of pigeons. A small white bird with a yellow plume on his head darts among them, stealing what he can.

The sun is lying on the canal where it widens in some dazzling way that reminds of a trip from years ago. Shana and I drove up to the lake above her house. We'd dipped our toes in the water, and she'd lain on top of me for hours, looking out over the water into the incandescent light of our futures.

"I'm going to be Buzz Aldrin," I'd said, watching leaves drop in lazy circles towards the water.

"Buzz Aldrin?"

"You know, the guy who almost made it to the moon," I said, rolling over, kissing the space on her skin where neck met shoulder.

"Couldn't you set your sights a little higher?" she asked, arching her eyebrows.

"Higher than the moon?" I asked, pinching her brown arm, still warm from summer light.

"Almost the moon," she said, giggling a little, and rolling onto her back and away from me. Her hair was wet, and her body was as thin as a reed. I do not know if anything in life will ever match that afternoon at the lake.

We walk down a tree-lined street scattered with yellow leaves. A statue of Garibaldi stands on a stone dais at the end of the street, circled by a black iron fence. Beneath the statue was a winged lion: the symbol of Venice. Garibaldi was covered in pigeons.

"They're shitting on the founder of Italy."

"Do something about it, then," Shana says, releasing my hand.

I run toward the pigeons, shouting, "I'm a scarecrow, you sons of bitches, be scared." The pigeons hop off the statue and drop into the street, standing dumbly among the leaves.

"Are you going to help?" I ask, and Shana shakes her head.

It's just me and Garibaldi now. His whole face is covered in white shit, and we stare at each other as though we are brothers. I slowly raise my hand and salute him.

By the time we leave, the pigeons are back on Garibaldi, shitting everywhere, because that's the way of the world.

Shana and I walk down the narrow, shaded streets of Venice towards squares of light. We pass small houses—water-damaged bricks, statues of women's heads, bouquets of flowers on the balcony—all that fading and decadent beauty. We cross little bridges over slow water and pass thousand-year-old buildings.

As we walk along the filthy canal, an aqueduct appears—the face of a lion—spitting water into a moss-encrusted basin. Shana puts her head underneath the spout and then her whole body. Her bra is visible, and her shirt cleaves to the small curve of her stomach. I put my head beneath the flowing water; it is clean and cold.

"I have been anointed," I say, slapping Shana's ass. She spits a mouthful of water in my face, and I grab her narrow hips and pull them towards me. We kiss like people who are still in love. I think that this moment is perfect, like when Buzz was watching Armstrong plant the flag on the moon. I wonder if he loved him from behind the glass of the shuttle window. We wrap our hands together like lovers.

We arrive back in St. Mark's Square with a thousand other tourists. The wind swirls, blows papers from the sky, catches and holds them. We stand in line for what feels like hours.

"We should talk some time," Shana says, bumping me with her hip, and smiling.

"What do you think we're doing?" I ask. "Exchanging guttural growls of apes?"

She lowers her eyes, and her shoulders drop.

Inside the basilica, we stand underneath the ceilings, incredibly vaulted like all the churches in Europe, and look at the Apostles and Disciples on the ceiling. I think of all those Apostles who spent their whole lives doing the right thing, and how they died just the same. And maybe Buzz had been jealous at the window, maybe he'd wished that Armstrong died.

We walk to the top of the building and stand on a balcony overlooking the courtyard. The wind blows trash from the square towards the canal, and Shana's nipples poke through her shirt. The pigeons and people flock to a patch of light in the center of the square. It is cold, and we stand together like that, just watching for a long time.

"Where did you go?" she asks. "I needed you that day. I don't know if I can ever forgive you for leaving." She keeps staring straight ahead though, watching light crumbling from the sky.

I remember the afternoon she told me about the miscarriage. She'd been crying in the bathroom, wanting me to hold her, but I'd left instead. I spent the afternoon in the park, drinking beer, watching kids play on swings and fall back and forth into the arms of their fathers, praying for no reason.

We look down at a three-pronged lamppost, pigeons winging above piles of trash. The sunlight starts to fade and everything—the water, the sky, the light—turns the shade of blue of Picasso's *The Old Guitarist*.

We walk across the square, still dotted with tourists. The smears of exhaust are cloaked in dark, and the buildings are like gargantuan sentries on some ancient Roman highway.

"Do you think we can still fix things?" Shana asks as we walk towards the sleek black gondolas that patrol Venice at night.

"I don't know a hell of a lot," I say, remembering how we'd talked about floating above all that dark water, above the bones of all the men who had built this dying city, how it would be like space. That it would be like traveling inside a black hole and looking back at the stars. How foolish we were, how foolish we have always been.

The gondolier has a tattoo on his right biceps that he flexes slightly as he smiles at both of us.

"How much?" Shana asks.

"Ninety," he answers, trying to catch her eye.

"I think we've got that much," she says, digging into the purse that I'd stolen hours earlier. She squeezes my hand as if to reassure me, and steps into the swaying gondola. And as she settles into the red satin interior, moonlight seems to be caught in strands of her hair.

The morning after I had built the crib, I wandered through the house in a vague green light towards a banging sound. I opened the bedroom door of my dear little boy, the one who I'd built the crib for, and there was Shana, smashing it with the end of a hammer. She was crying, and I wanted to hold her. I wanted that shuttle to pierce the veil of clouds and drift off into the dark cold of space where we could be alone.

"What the hell are you doing?" I asked, trying to grab the hammer from her shaking hands. She leaned forward and sobbed into my chest. I stroked her hair and held her tightly against my chest. But no, that never happened. I walked away then, too.

The moonlight has left her hair. I run as fast as my legs will carry me, and it feels as though I am the wind, as if I am faster than the sound of her voice. I run through the square and into the side streets, heart pounding, shoes burning. I run through the night until I reach an empty street lined by flowers. The crickets are silent. I stand on a bridge overlooking dark water, which reflects the stars. It feels good to be alone again. Perhaps that is all any of us are fit for.

The sky turns black, and I am in a steady rain. I walk down a narrow street—exposed brick, graffiti, bits of trash and puddles, a pink checkered dress blowing in the wind and rain. The stars are dead things hidden by a curtain of clouds. We are all empty planets in space separated by fathomless darkness, and it's a miracle, like this city of water or the flag on the moon, that two people ever understand each other.

The rain is starting to freeze. A stray dog—thin slats for ribs—licks water from where it collects between stones. I walk down the wide tree-lined street, and the branches bend in the wind, pointing me toward Garibaldi. I stand in the dark at the foot of the statue, watching it rain.

"I'm sorry," I say, to the statue. I lift my arm to salute him for a second time. I shiver; rain runs down both our faces, falling from our chins. Here we are, me and my shat-upon brother, standing in the rain, waiting to come clean.

BEING AND TIME

The differences between God and humans are as manifold as human's wickedness. One can make a cup of His hand and swing it through the dark ink of the sky as if it were water, disturbing the constellations, scattering Ursa Major, or pulling comets by their tails across the Milky Way. The other can only gaze up at the stars on a clear night, and ponder, in that silence, all the space between things, the way that stars sometimes brighten and then go dark. There are so many differences that I could write for as long as the universe spins out galaxies, the variety of O's: omnipotent, omniscient, etc., but the difference that's relevant to my own story is that God lives outside of time, flashing in and out of it like a sun-warmed bather by the pool. Man, bound to time, is forever entangled in the world: in petty jealousies, toenail clippings, erecting of shelter, the raising and shearing of sheep, the finding and losing of a wife or husband, connecting the wires on a television, yelling at a neighbor, burning a dinner of salmon and rice, vaguely noting a distant war, smoking a cigarette on the porch while the wind blows softly through trees emulating the ocean. God is capable of constructing a universe. Man can only create small things—a statue, a blueberry pie, an essay, a kitchen garden, a parking ticket—meager offerings in the face of the cosmos.

~

In the early days, not every rule had been carved into stone tablets, which meant that some of us, who weren't quite defined, lived outside of time. God hadn't thought through the logistics of everything yet. God was always more of a brass-tacks kind of person. We spent a great deal of time, which is oxymoronic, playing chess. Chess can be interminably boring. However, unmoored from time, the game became a wonder. Once, while considering a move for one of my knights, I paused and looked at the dust motes floating over my water and then took a drink. When I looked beyond the board to the world, I saw that dinosaurs were now extinct, a continent had broken free from its shelf, and small animals were scurrying between caves. I looked at my opponent, but He hadn't noticed a thing, engrossed as he was in Alekhine's gun. God was, for all intents and purposes, a dismal chess player.

I realize that my description of God and time doesn't really make sense to a person in your present state, situated in time, reading on a couch—a computer warm in your lap—or scrolling on a phone, or watching a movie, or standing at the sink, gazing dully at the dishes. Or at least I'm not very good at it. Describing it to you accurately would be akin to teaching your dog to read from the Vulgate in perfect Latin. Dogs are notoriously dismal at Latin.

~

During those later days, if later is what they were, when we'd stopped playing chess, we'd watch people moving through the world, out of what would now be called Africa and into the great unknown, though we had a pretty good idea of the geography. Perspective is everything, and we could already see that they'd eventually cover the Earth. Down below, the people moved as quickly as a shaft of light through stained glass. And yet, at some moments, we would sit and contemplate every pore on someone's skin, a birthmark on their right elbow in the shape of the Adriatic, a crow's foot, the slight fold of skin on their knuckles as they reached towards a pear, breaking a small spider's web with their left forefinger.

But the watching began to change the way I related to the people below, who before had been abstractions, like shadows thrown upon a wall. Now I could see a bit of what He saw in them, their fragility, the way their bones broke, and the way they cried so often when they were alone, such tenderness, such love. We didn't have the equivalent, nothing of the feeling of loss that accompanied their lives. None of us had ever stood in the backyard and buried our new child. There were no children among us, we people of the sky. I could see the piercing beauty of sheaths of corn blowing in a steady wind, the sky overhead electric blue. I believe this time of close observation is what led me into the disaster, if loving an ephemeral thing is a disaster, and I now believe it to be. How much easier it is to love the divine, the unchanged and unchangeable. Humans wriggle around like snakes.

I don't remember the precise year that I fell in love. The women were wearing short skirts then and dainty shoes. They were taken to dancing in groups late at night, shaking their hips as if they were tribal women in the early days, trying to keep warm. The woman I fell in love with, a whip-smart divorcee of thirty-two, was eating frozen blueberries on a blanket by the river, watching the underside of leaves reflecting geometries of light. I don't know if she was thinking then of her children, or her ex-husband, or nothing at all, but I could see in the pensive look, the slight mark between her eyebrows, something in need of love. Or perhaps it was I that was in need of love, run dry like a desert culvert after all those years in the sky. I tucked my terrible wings inside a suit coat and started talking fast about tax law and my dreams of the sky, of the songs of certain birds and the color of the top of rainbows. It took me a while to get the hang of how to talk to someone ensconced in time, mired in the muck of day-to-day life.

In the beginning, we talked often of our hopes and dreams, which centered on the dividends from her 401K and the ability of her children to get scholarships to four-year colleges or maybe spend a year or two at the local junior college and then transfer elsewhere. It concerned her that I didn't have a job, and she pestered me frequently about my working resume and the long gap between employments. Those were halcyon days, just after we'd met when I tethered myself to her and felt as if I finally existed as a part of time.

It felt as though this time could last forever. I found everything she did enchanting, the way she sometimes spit water when she laughed, her small vanities, her inability to cook a roast without burning it, her love of roses.

Our happiness could not, as I'm sure you've already guessed, last. We had a logistical problem, which was the fundamentally different way that we experienced time. Sometimes she'd asked me to meet her at the Italian restaurant on Thursday night at 7 p.m., and I'd want to oblige her. And yet, as soon as I left her, I'd lose track of things and end up arriving days early or late. And I'd show up at the restaurant and listen to the songbirds in the trees or the pawing of the rain on the rooftop, growing angrier at her, until I checked my phone, and figured out that it was I who'd made the mistake. And so when we finally did meet we'd haggle over minor things like whether we wanted the duck confit or the braised veal, each of us assuming that the other was in some way choosing the dish not out of a desire for it but as a means of punishing the other.

~

Our further undoing was that our relationship coincided with Gabriel reminding us of the good old days before we had humans to watch, when we'd play chess. And I felt within myself a quiet stirring, like wind upon a room full of dust, a longing for the game when we'd yell, "Rook 8 to Pawn 2." We were inveterate jokesters when it came to chess and meant nothing by our yelling as we barely understood the pieces, which sometimes disintegrated in the long stretch of time in between our moves, until we wound up moving bits of dust with our fingernails across the oak board, breathing softly, quietly, in an attempt to not lose everything.

Unfortunately, now engrossed in these games, I sometimes wouldn't check on her for a week or two. And when I finally did, she pointed out that my absences made her feel vulnerable and self-conscious and reminded her of her ex-husband, who was a bit of a layabout. And didn't I know she had kids? She counted on me to show up because she had to arrange babysitters for these nights out and lay out explicit directions for how and when to serve meals, all at the end of a long week that had already left her feeling ragged and in need of a good scream. And then when I didn't show up, it made her question what she was up to, working long hours, making sure the children had vegetables with every meal, were clean and well-adjusted, if only to carve out two hours in her life to meet with someone who didn't give a damn about her. That she was right was insufficient. I could not tie myself to her or the children; such a thing was not allowed.

We spent a day I remember in the Green Mountains of Vermont. We walked through a field where the bluebells, clover, and dandelions covered the hillside like a quilt. The sky suddenly darkened, voluminous clouds appeared, and we hid beneath the eaves of a large pine while hailstones fell around us like the wrath of God. Later, the sun appeared, and we finished our hike to a waterfall. We read passages to one another from Hemingway's *The Sun Also Rises* while sitting on a blanket, the spray of the fall nearly reaching our faces, falling down on the rocks, creating rainbows in the air. A pair of black swifts harvested insects, dark blurs against the paler bruise of the sky. She lay back in my arms; her hair smelled of apples. She said that she wished the moment could last forever. And I became aware suddenly of time, time washing over me, filling me, every crevice, in my nose and eyes, time pouring out of me like sand from a glass. And I saw that time could consume me. Or I thought I did, for suddenly that afternoon flowed away like leaves in autumn wind, her children grew up and left her, and I disappeared for a decade by accident, and she was soon dead. Perhaps I understood nothing.

Here is what she could have meant by time—time is something that you can scoop into your hands, like God with a sky full of stars, or a child with fine grains of sand. Time is like a shark, either moving or dead. Time is the soft feeling on the inside of her palm, my finger running along a spidery blue vein, tracing it back toward the heart along a hand suddenly covered in wrinkles. Time is that which does not stop.

Long after the stars have stopped their idle burning and turned to dust, I'll be sitting in an ever-darkening room, watching time lap at the window like water on a shore. In the mornings, I'll think of her, the crow's feet on her eyes, the steel gray of her hair, her slender fingers, this woman, dead now for a week, a day, or a millennium. I was just telling God the other day that I don't understand time, and God pointed out that when it comes to brass tacks, I don't really understand much of anything. God said time was like a mustard seed, like the birds of the field, and then God trailed off and looked for a long time at the universe in a deep well of silence.

Perhaps it's blasphemy to say it, but I hope when the universe is ripped to shreds that I go with it.

God and I are playing chess. We're using the stars as pawns, moons as rooks, planets as knights, suns as bishops, and galaxies as kings and queens. Sometimes I look away in my reverie, and I swear that God has moved another piece across the vast black space of sky, cheating once again, while I ponder my next move.

OF LAKES AND SWANS

My daughter likes me to tell her stories before bed. She keeps quiet as I try to weave something meaningful with words, her eyebrows knitted in concentration. Being a parent in the evening is wretched—arguments over bowel movements, hallway lights and the angles of doors fill your time when you desperately want them to sleep. And yet, this evening, with the lamp turned low, I begin to tell her a story.

Some time ago there was a duchess who lived on the shores of a lake. The lake was formed during the period when glaciers started to melt, leaving behind large swaths of water in declivities, or so the duchess read in a book from the library. In the evenings, moonlight threaded through the water, and she'd watch patterns of light from a large bay window that overlooked the lake and trees. If the evening was warm, she'd open the window and listen to the boughs of the trees bending in the wind.

During the colder months, she'd keep the window closed, but she often leaned against it, letting the chill suffuse her body. She found herself wishing she could take flight to somewhere warmer. She was lonely, which is not an unusual condition in this fairy tale or life.

The duchess often saw a black swan swimming on the lake, visible through the limbs of beech and bays. The swan arrived early in the evening, from sky to water, spreading its wings as it settled—beads of water fanning out like mist. The swan glided along as the evening blued, and dragonflies whirred in the gloaming. The duchess watched the swan with the intensity that a child loves their first blanket or a parent's voice.

There was also, in this strange land, a Komodo dragon, who slipped through the cattails to stand on the shores of the lake, his claws gripping the peat moss. The Komodo dragon was not conventionally beautiful, which he understood as he gazed at his reflection; small eddies of wind blew across his scales, leaving him cold as he watched the swan and himself. He knew that something divided the swan and him that went beyond scales and feathers.

He saw that the swan was lovely, an aesthetic marvel, and he wanted to emulate that beauty. He understood that as a Komodo dragon, his perspective on the world was circumscribed: hunt, poison, death, a terrible rhythm. And he wasn't sure how he would go about capturing the beauty that he saw in the sway of the swan's neck, the way that water left in her wake moved like the pattern of dreams.

The Komodo dragon didn't understand boundaries and stared at the swan for hours. And finally, the Komodo dragon decided that the way to possess beauty was to kill her. He understood that this action fulfilled a narrative function that was deeply troubling to his self-conception as an individual capable of transcendence. And yet, it occurred to him that perhaps eating the swan, feeling the lightness of her bones in his belly, was the only way that he'd ever fully comprehend her and achieve transcendence, so he slipped into the water.

The lonely duchess heard an insistent pounding at her door, shaking her from her reverie. As she looked out she wondered how she'd gotten into the house with the bay window, wondered why she was alone. Didn't she have some friends who would stop by and drink rosé before falling asleep to a movie? She couldn't remember if she was paying a fifteen- or thirty-year mortgage. In fact, who owned the house, anyway? Perhaps the person who was banging at the door and yelling her name, if it was her name. Was her name Penelope? What a silly name that was. She didn't know why her wardrobe consisted only of white frilly dresses. Why was the door to the house always locked? Who brought the food that she ate each evening?

Her heart pounded. The thumping at the door was insistent; she heard glass being smashed and someone fumbling with the lock. She frantically looked out at the Komodo dragon, who was making his way towards the swan with dogged strokes. The duchess locked her door.

Then the duchess came to a very strange realization. She wasn't a woman standing at a window. Rather, she was the swan swimming in the lake and also the woman. How she could simultaneously be a woman staring down at a swan by the lake and also that swan itself is beyond the scope of what I can explain in the short amount of time we have together. Needless to say, identity is fluid rather than fixed.

Whoever it was at the door had gotten in; the duchess heard footsteps on the lower level of the house and someone still shouting her name.

If I were to read into it, I'd say that this story is a bit about possession and perhaps sexual power dynamics, but also about beauty and freedom and maybe identity formation.

Anyhow, upon realizing that she was a swan, the duchess wondered what she should do. The footsteps stopped at her door and the pounding was now there. She saw the Komodo dragon doggedly churning water, now only a few feet from the swan. The wind whipped through the trees, and white curtains billowed, as white curtains do, and the duchess, knowing now what she should do, stepped into the windowpane, her toes gripping the ledge as she stood, and then jumped. The house that possessed her and the voice that called for her could no longer contain her. She belonged to the lakes and skies now.

She was going to fly forever. She was going to pierce the veil of heaven. She was going to soar up into the clouds and spread her arms out wide, feel the moisture washing across her fingertips. But first, all she felt was the sensation of falling.

IT RAINED LAUGHTER

We were busy women who worked long days in gray office buildings downtown—buildings that cast shadows over park squares, where crows nibbled shiny bits of trash and homeless men slept their restless sleep on benches. After our last meetings finished and we'd sent an email to remind ourselves of all the things left to do, we slipped hats and coats on over our dresses or suits and went on long elevator rides to the bottom floor, our faces slack, absent, and then out the glass doors into a brisk wind that flowed through the long caverns between office buildings and into the blued dusk of early evening. We were late to see our husbands and children. We cursed our luck, our high mortgage rates, and we called our husbands and told them to kiss the children on their sweet foreheads in case we didn't make it home.

We worked long hours to keep them happy—the cherub-cheeked children, the sweet husbands who tended to cinnamon rolls on Saturday mornings with all the care and attention that we wished we gave our children. We were tired and worried about our careers, our overbearing bosses, our meetings with clients, with contractors and sub-contractors. We worried whether we were good mothers, whether the store-bought cake we'd purchased had high-fructose corn syrup as an ingredient. We worried about juice boxes and goldfish and the presentation of women in *Sofia the First*. We worried about whether our children were writing well. Were most kids still drawing P's backward? We worried whether they were reading well and cutting with scissors in an age-appropriate manner. We worried about our husbands. Had they gotten too boring? Had we?

Sometimes we'd see a slip of moon hung in the velvety sky, and we'd find ourselves crying for no good reason, or maybe every reason that we could think of. Sometimes we steeled ourselves against the imploring looks of our husbands as we stared at our phones during dinner; we steeled ourselves against the complaints of our children, their questions and inanities, against their oatmeal-covered hands, against the narrow contours of a life.

In the driveway, we looked in compact mirrors, wiped away tears, smoothed brows, and composed our faces into the shapes that our families wanted from us. We were so happy to see them and so tired to the marrow. We felt fissures forming deep inside us.

One day in early April, a springtime day of flowing skirts, purple crocuses, and barrel-chested robins digging in the grass, when we were winding down conference calls, closing computers, putting on jackets, fielding calls from anxious nannies or husbands about the balance in the checking account, about a grocery list, about whether pennies were digestible, about a strange-looking rash on a child's lower back, it began to rain laughter.

At first, from inside office buildings, we weren't sure what was happening in the streets; it started with a fine mist of giggles, very soft and sweet. Some of us looked into the sky where fat purple clouds hung. Others looked around with smiles of wonderment as the laughter began to build. We heard peals of laughter that reminded us of videos of our mothers, taken when we were babies, our mothers' faces, so smooth, so young. We heard bells of laughter that reminded us of our childhoods, spinning in circles and blowing spores of dandelions in fields of dry grass, and still, the laughter continued, becoming the deep-throated guffaws of long-dead grandfathers, who sat on porches and told us stories of fairies and angels. We heard the surprisingly high-pitched titter of long-forgotten college lovers and the sharp intake of breath that preceded the laughter of a friend we'd lost touch with and who had died suddenly last year of ovarian cancer. By then, the laughter was falling all around us, merriment dripping from the limbs of elm trees. A giggle was traveling around and around a fountain in the park; a raucous laugh fell down the stairs towards the subway. There was wild laughter gathering in gutters and chortles falling on the windows of coffee shops. There was a whoop of laughter that bent the tops of trees.

And for once, we paused our busy lives to hear it. We put away our phones, our thoughts of Google calendars, parent-teacher conferences, doctor's appointments and 403 B's. We got off trains, stepped out of coffee shops, called meetings short and stood, eyes brimming with delight. We took our coffee cups and handbags into the street and gathered the laughter we found in the tangled roots of trees. We gathered it from beneath awnings and from the underside of iron chairs. We captured it in the tops of our hats and in every jacket pocket. We cupped our hands together and held laughter there. We chased bubbly laughter down the street. We found gales of laughter gathered in a depression on Fifth Avenue.

Finally, the storm passed, and we got back into our cars, back onto trains, and went home. We came in the door bursting with laughter; we held giggles to our children's ears and showered wild, cackling laughter on our husbands. We fell on the floor, all together, in a river of laughter. We found in that sudden storm a small filling for the cracks forming inside us, and for an evening, we were as happy as we'd been in years.

MAYBE THIS TIME

Maybe this time she won't start texting in the middle of the night, her fingers moving across the keys of her phone like wind in trees, face a halo of electric light. Maybe this time I'll come home from work early and slip into the evening routine like slippers instead of kissing her lips, parted in a smile. Maybe this time we'll travel to Spain—roseate bull rings, the sword, and the cape, and afterward, the thin tongue of the silver glass holding wine, cockles simmering in broth, anything but the monotony of here and now. Maybe we'll be there instead of arguing over contributions to the Roth IRA, to the thrift savings retirement plan, to saving everything for another day, another month, another life we are waiting to live.

Maybe this time we'll travel to Maine, folding and unfolding the map as we try and find ourselves on the spidery back roads, fingers tracing the thin lines like a lover along a wrist's vein. And we'll lie in a hammock up north, beneath a thick blue sky, listening to a woodpecker hammering rhythmically into a half-dead alder, and I'll massage her slim feet, rolling my thumbs along the arches, while she tells me about her job tending to children, dabbing noses with Kleenex and teaching them to slide their finger across the letters, how to recognize the arrival of a soft e. Maybe this time she'll tell me about a summer from her childhood out West when she swung across the blue mirror of water in the tire swing, the arc something we could find using a cosine or a tangent. And then the moment, nothing mathematical about it, when she'd wriggle free from the black belt of tire, not knowing if she'd land on the rocks or the water, falling ass-over-ankles into the unknown.

Maybe this time we'll adopt a cat with gray fur the sooty color of every cold winter day in the city. And we'll watch him scurry from bed to pillow to curtain, claws flexing and unflexing like a flower opening and closing in harmony with light. Maybe this time we'll play hide-and-go-seek, and I'll slip into the darkness like a stone into water, until I am absorbed by it, underneath the bed, stifling a laugh. Maybe this time I'll burst out laughing as I grab her leg from underneath the bed, and she'll scream, and we'll both forget ourselves, our goddamn grasping selves.

Maybe this time we'll play croquet and drink wine coolers, while the mosquitoes swarm above tufts of fescue that are pointless because between dandelion spores, the wind, and the oak, nothing but mosquitoes grow well here. Maybe this time we'll be better at telling our friends we miss them, crafting long emails and short postcards from Maine, from Spain, from the patio. Maybe we'll have sex on the kitchen table, sex against the window, sex on a Tuesday afternoon, sex again on the table, and we'll finally break the legs off that goddamn wobbly thing, and we'll collapse onto the floor, and we'll lie, sweat rimming our lips, just like that, me inside you. We won't start scrolling through our phones, desperately searching for Craigslist ads within a five-mile radius, trying to calculate the cost of renting a U-Haul, or wondering about a friend with a truck who could possibly help if we asked, instead, we'll lie in parabolas of salt, counting the ribs of light passing through the blinds.

Maybe this time she won't gather up the books one morning—Borges, Calvino, Tolstoy, Munro—in a box that seems impossibly small for the capaciousness of their thoughts. Maybe this time she'll listen to me when I tell her about the story I was reading about multiple personalities and infinity, while the moon bobs in the faraway sky, orbiting us through the trees, thinking moon thoughts, quiet and lunar.

Maybe this time we won't cry on the couch beneath the window where I once watched snow pile in drifts, trying to recall the exact shape of our love, the words we used, the gestures, when we were so much younger and made up of entirely different atoms.

Maybe this time my father will love me exactly as I would have liked, and I won't spend years chasing him like a ghost story, only to find him staring at me in the bathroom mirror. And we'll read that poem by Philip Larkin at the beginning of our marriage instead of the end, and we'll know what signs to look for, like fissures in the cracked earth; we'll look for the math in everything; love in everything; art in everything; we'll think of the arc and curve of the water as it fell from the balcony decades ago, the two of us at play.

Maybe this time we'll learn to play backgammon instead of staring at the diagonal slashes like lightning, thinking it obscure, confusing. Maybe this time our lives will start to become more cohesive, instead of sliding further and further apart, like the universe, and it will all make sense instead of being a collection of memories, yellowed in time, afternoons by the water feeding ducks wafer-thin crackers, petty disappointments of any old day or life.

Maybe this time we'll build a boat before the storm, before the rain falls in sheets, covering the green fields, the bits of black-eyed Susans, lavender, rosemary, and rotting tomatoes that make up the yard. We can load at least two of every animal, and every couple we know, and we'll stay on the boat while the water rises around us, like dreams, like an angel, something to lift us up onto a mountain that God will call good.

Or maybe this time we'll just go back to sleep, we'll just cry, maybe this time will be like every other time that our knees touched on the blanket beneath the couch, yet another beginning to an end.

COME WINTER

The slender streetlamps illuminate the banks of snow on street corners. Icicles are forming under the eaves. In the distance, garbage trucks grind over the ice and salt. But it's warm in the study, where I have patiently been writing you for months. I turn a page in my journal and run my fingers along the ridges of a pencil. I write to you of the shades of snow, from purest white of first fall to the corroded black after exhaust, dirt, and time have passed. I write to you of how the maple tree on Forty-Fifth turned first, red and brilliant against barren autumnal skies. I write to you when I am tired or confused, or pensive. In short, I write you.

In winter, the clouds seem cruel and thick, though I know that clouds are nonentities, incapable of cruelty, and that it's just a mood I'm in. I miss and think of you often. Why don't you join me this winter and explain the differences among clouds—cirrus, contrails, orographic, and cumulus? I'd listen to you as if I were a small child, sleepy and indulgent, content to have the world constructed for me by your voice. Our days would be like this: You sit in the window and read a book, while I read on the bed. When we are bored with the books we are reading, we'll look out the window and talk about the people walking by. We'll describe their interior lives, children, pets, and loves, and then we'll forget them and kiss.

The letters aren't all strange like that. Most of them are mundane. I'll tell you about the new goldfish I bought, Henry, who is so silent, or the notes of a Bach piece that slip through the wall. Sometimes I'll tell you the truth and write: I am lonely; I am lonely; I am lonely. And then I stop. I remind myself that this feeling will pass, as every feeling passes. That you, too, will someday pass from my mind, like a meteor burning through the night sky, brief and brilliant, then gone.

This winter I plan to forget you. Life is full of failed projects. I painted a picture of you on my wall instead. I am a poor painter and got all the details wrong. Your lips are thinner and pinker than the ones in my picture. Your hair has shades of red that I cannot capture. I could not remember the color of your fingernails. How strange it is to have forgotten anything about you. I wonder what you'd think of this painting, of this early winter snow, of damn near everything.

Just the other day, I read that the universe might be infinite. And it almost comforted me to think of the endless chances we'd have if that were true. Surely in one of them your fingernails would be drumming along my spine, keeping time with the snow and the Bach. I don't believe the universe is infinite. I believe this is our only chance to go about the messy business of life.

THE NOTE

We took a taxi to the airport early in the morning. The orange sky rose behind the bare limbs of trees so that they appeared to be a grove of something in wild bloom. The drive was quick and without much to report on at that time of day—rows of houses, Victorian, bungalow, and craftsman—eventually giving way to apartment buildings as we neared the freeway. When we reached the airport, you got out quickly, and I sensed the anticipation in your body, nearly throbbing to leave me. At the edge of the curb, you pulled me to you, smelling of my wintergreen detergent, and the two of us hugged very closely as though we were lovers parting for a short time, rather than for good. You said many sweet things as you ran your fingers through my hair, but I was captivated by a small blemish on the sidewalk, perhaps left by a piece of gum that had been ground underfoot many times. Or was it something else? Maybe the paint from a black suitcase, scuffed as someone ran into the airport. I became interested in the shape of the object, while you whispered how much you'd miss me in France, at your new university, which was a lie, but one that neither one of us bothered acknowledging. You'd lose yourself in language, in coffee shops, in talks of Foucault and Derrida, in a swirl of catlike female faces.

But I digress. What I became captivated with was not necessarily the spot itself, but its shape, which exactly replicated, in precise detail, the contours of the state of California. I found that as I ignored your voice, I smelled the apple orchards that I'd traversed in my youth, that I saw the spindles of light and the green leaves on the stems. I saw the wrinkles in my Aunt Evie's face, almost like a sail billowing in the wind. How could a shape on the cement smell like California? I didn't know, so I tried to banish you as quickly as possible, knowing that this next journey wouldn't need you at all. For the first time, it was you who was crying, not me.

Back home, I noticed that the world had started to shift around me. I found myself regarding a bit of soap scum, greenish-white, gathered at the edge of the dish in my shower, and I tasted suddenly the salty air of Fort Bragg, from a trip I'd taken with my mother and siblings to the coast when I was a child. We'd walked among the flowers and thistle on the dirt paths that ran along the cliffs, pulling fat, fuzzy caterpillars from long blades of grass. Then we'd hurled them into the air and watched their bodies curl up and then lift off in a gust of wind, on their way to becoming butterflies a bit too early.

This newfound sensation, the world unfurling like a map before me as though I were a cartographer of sensations, was deeply unnerving and freeing. I saw a fly buzzing in a window, and I swear I'd it seen before, during a sticky summer day in Mexico when I'd been on my honeymoon. This same fly alighted on the rim of my margarita glass at a restaurant outside Cancun, where a band of mariachis was flailing away. My husband was asleep on the narrow table after becoming dehydrated

on a hike, and the rain thrashed at the roof. And this fly
and I stood witness to the first cracks.

It was as though the code of the world, which is
mathematical, had suddenly been revealed to me.
Everything was a revelation. And so I decided to write a
note to you, about what I've been feeling this last month
while you've been kissing graduate students in France.
The note was handwritten, and I only used the margins
because I saw in the white-lined space of the page a
memory of childhood, a time my mother had taken
us up into the snow because we'd all been acting like
hellions on the way to church. We'd thrown snowballs at
one another and laughed all afternoon, the sunlight on
the snow blinding. I didn't want to deface the memory.
And then I tore off the strip of what I'd written and
stared it for a long time, waiting for the world to reveal
itself to me.

After a while, I realized that nothing was going to
change this time, so I started taking tiny slips of paper
and eating them. You'll be surprised to know that I's taste
best. They have a distinct flavor of iced tea and bring
to mind screened porches, lemonade, and the sound of
crickets. D's are reminiscent of the crooked slant of old
tombstones in a graveyard. I picked up each letter that
had been torn, sampling the zesty E's, which are like the
sound of ice hitting a carbonated drink midsummer on
the coast of New England, like a host of gnats gathered
around a light near a softball field. I can tell you that L's
are like the streak of gray across the body of a house

wren, perched on a telephone wire in early spring, in an apartment you live in alone and divorced. Every letter, every bit of the world, is just a memory, an impression, a secret waiting to be unlocked.

I still remember sitting in the car, thinking of California and watching your plane take off. It wasn't your plane, of course, but one of the ten to fifteen that were given clearance as my car sat in the dense traffic on the freeway now, but I imagined it was—contrails cutting like a knife through the blue sky, and the plane a blue freight train, a caterpillar, then a bullet, then a butterfly, then nothing at all.

DREAM MOTHER

He and his dead mother were walking along a slender path lined by yews, limbs swathed in moss. Opposite lay a boundary wall of large, flat gray stones, dragged from the ground and set out to mark the fields that were now mostly overtaken by forest. The man was wearing sensible shoes, and the light was pleasant and warm. They were chatting about the dinner they'd had—a chicken stuffed with garlic and potatoes, and biscuits peppered with scallions. They enjoyed these intimate talks after dinner when both of them were full and content. The heat was diminishing, and the wind was very light and blowing from the southwest. At times, patches of blackberries appeared at path's edge, dangling and sumptuous.

She was dead, yes, but they didn't talk about it. It would have made the conversation awkward, made the distance between them seem insurmountable. In the old fields, where gardens had once been planted—tomatoes, carrots, chives—the two of them could see starlings flitting through the yews, like a hailstorm of darkness. As they walked, he thought of how lonely he was in his apartment, but he didn't tell her. Some things you keep from mothers for fear of worrying them, even dead ones.

Besides, his mother had always suspected he'd end up lonely after the acrimonious divorce he had with his wife. The divorce had been difficult for his mother. For him, it had been an improvement, but he understood his own needs were secondary to hers. She'd had such high hopes for him. She had also gotten divorced, but she had never wanted that for her children, she said. As though anyone would wish hardship on their children. Mothers sometimes spoke in platitudes.

When they'd talk on the phone in the years following, he could feel the weight of her disappointment in the silences she often slipped into. Sometimes she sighed deeply on the phone, and when he asked after her sigh, she said it was nothing.

When she was feeling well, instead of rebuking him with her silence and sighs, his mother would talk of her cats, Bootsy and Mink, a calico and a Manx. The cats were indoor/outdoor and terrorized the neighborhood bird population. She had a deep love for her cats; it was almost ineffable. Once, Bootsy had gone missing for two days, and his mother had been hysterical. She'd called him and his sister, desperate for help. As he drove across town, passing apartment buildings and ivy-covered yards, he felt a deep well of anger rising in him. His mother had never been that frantic about her children. He was wrong about this, of course, but he couldn't see into the past, glimpse her sleep-addled brain, or remember the fifty times she'd leaned over during the first weeks of his life, placing her small hand on his chest, desperate to feel the breath push the small slats of his ribs up.

Once, he sent her an article on Facebook about the incredible detriment to the environment outdoor cats can be. He felt passionate about birds, National Parks. She never responded, but when she wanted to talk to him, she started a new thread.

Sometimes they argued about the cats, about birds and politics. His mother was far more right-leaning than he was, though she seemed unable to articulate why. She just was. Mostly, he listened to her chatter. In her final years, she had taken a deep and abiding interest in her cats, her watercolor class and her son. She was a real talker, his still-living mother.

Death had softened her a bit. Sometimes they walked in silence, through bars of light flickering through the trees. And he appreciated the silence because it was no longer a rebuke, but an expression of comfort. He didn't feel moved to tell her about his life. Rather, the two of them basked in the silence, in the comfort of presence, like a mother with her newborn. Sometimes he wished his mother had always been dead.

In the years before the cats, his mother had taken several lovers. She didn't like being lonely. It took her some time to figure out houseplants, and cats were considerably less trouble than men. One of the men had been depressed; another, a philanderer. The last had given a thousand dollars of their shared money to a televangelist. When she'd discovered this, she'd gone out driving, wondering what to do as sunset pierced the sky and filled the spaces between eucalyptus trees with absurd and pointless beauty. Who was this meant for? She'd driven and driven until she'd passed an animal shelter and that had been that. Bootsy didn't care for television or religion as far as she could tell, which suited her just fine. Mink had come along later, and her tastes were harder to define, but that was another story.

How she had come to be dead is a topic they also assiduously avoided, in the way some children avoid vegetables. He suspected she had died of a heart attack, but he felt he couldn't ask her without being rude. Her skin had a yellow pallor, and her fingers tightened on his elbow when the path grew steeper as though she was laboring while climbing, which seemed implausible. But it turned out the dead got tired, too. The roots of the trees were reminiscent of knobby knuckles, and he appreciated the symmetry between her hands and the roots. It reminded him of some of the watercolors she'd done in her declining years. Or maybe it didn't. The details of her paintings were fuzzy. Either way, he liked the correspondence he had never found in his life, which was like the stainless-steel ball, whacked round in a pinball machine, bouncing between this and that.

He wondered if his mother were a figment of his imagination, clothed in flesh by his dream, or whether it was his mother's spirit joining him as she slept, too. He didn't ask her the delicate question. It wasn't the sort of thing a son should be asking a mother, whether she was real or not. It would upset the tender balance of the mother-to-son relationship.

The dreamscape was strange, which was a bit like saying water was wet. Often, he saw other sons walking with their dead mothers, burnishing the roots with their footfalls. Some of the sons and mothers seemed to be very natural, leaned together on the curves, dead mothers laughing quickly at a shared joke. He didn't have those kinds of dreams where you could fly or realize you were dreaming and start killing everyone with impunity. Rather, his dreams pulled him along like a tunnel, like a dark subterranean river, like time.

The walk back to the graveyard was long enough for them to chat about this and that. She was asking him how he'd coped the year after his father left. He told her he remembered throwing a baseball against the garage over and over, bending and fielding it before firing it back into the door. He said that the rhythm brought him comfort, knowing that some things always return. But really, he would have been fine anyway. He just liked the image of the boy in the fading daylight, moths beginning to gather by the garage lights, throwing the ball over and over in the encroaching dark.

He had always been a dreamer, and of late, a fatalist. He felt as though his life, with all its cracks and failings, like an old Roman wall, was as it should be. He couldn't articulate why, but perhaps it was another expression of his intense passivity. He no longer believed that life was for the doers, but rather, that life happened either way.

That's good, his mother said when he'd finished the story about the ball and the garage. I worried about you so much.

I worried about you, too.

The repetition made them feel companionable. He had always yearned for a deep connection with his mother, but one had never materialized. The walk had a purpose. He was taking her back to her grave, where she usually slept in a patch of wet leaves next to her headstone.

When they reached the graveyard, he pushed back the iron gate with rusty hinges. Their feet crushed clover. Wrens were singing jumbly bits of song from nests in nearby oaks. The oaks plundered the soil for nutrients from the bodies of the dead. The headstones were slowly being pushed up, conducting their own mini-resurrections, and the light had dimmed, and now appeared more as a suggestion of light than the real thing.

She asked after his children, and he talked with her about their summer plans to visit Tucson and take a trip north to see Monument Valley. He was quite interested in sandstone formations, gorgeous and strange. He liked to look at glyphs and watch his children fighting in the back seat. He saw them so rarely that it wouldn't bother him. His dream mother didn't interrupt, though he could see she was growing tired and wanted to sleep.

Eventually, the two of them said goodbye, and he already felt himself missing his dream mother, who was such a patient listener even when he rambled on about the children's school projects and the way time and wind worked on rock. She was the mother he hadn't ever had in life. And he fought to stay in the dream, sitting by the headstones in the dark.

Once, when he was very young, his mother had left the water boiling on the stove, and he'd flipped the kettle over, spilling hot water over his left forearm. His arm had been badly burned, and he remembered his mother staying awake all night, cradling him as he cried. It was the closest he'd ever felt to her.

Each time he woke from these dreams of his mother, it took him a while to collect himself, to feel the press of the pillow in the curve of his neck, to make out the fan blades above him, gently stirring the air. And then, more often than not, he cried for his mother softly in the dark as if he were a child again, longing for his mother asleep in the next room.

THINGS SHE'S TIRED
OF HEARING

1. There are plenty of fish in the sea.

Who's to say fish would be any better than your garden-variety human at communicating over the nuances of a *Gilmore Girls* episode, building a dresser from IKEA, or talking about performing the self via Bakhtin?

There are plenty of fish in the sea, but their variety and form far surpasses that of humans, who sometimes speak different languages and eat different foods, and who might, if one doesn't look carefully, appear to be as varied as the fish in the sea. But, upon closer inspection, humans are narrower, more alike in nature and in kind than the cuttlefish harvesting crabs and the large checkerboard back of a whale shark, forty-feet long and docile as a cow. You will meet no human like the Mexican cavefish, who swims without eyes because eyes are too biologically expensive. Although she thinks, perhaps there is something to learn there with that fish, if only humans could give up the idea of love when it doesn't suit them, she'd shed it like eyes. But, she thinks, we haven't all the time of a cavefish, playing round in the low-oxygen dark with nothing better to do than evolve without sight. We have only these brief and scattered lives, which break like light on water.

2. But, you're such a catch.

Stop extending fishing metaphors to these people. Single people are mostly environmentalists. They don't want to hear about the ocean as though it's an underwater sexual playground.

As a child, at summer camp, far from home in upstate New York, she'd fallen in love with a boy, freckled and red-haired. The camp was alive with the sound of thrush and kinglet, alive with the shrieks and laughter of children, throwing acorns, cannonballing into the pond. One afternoon, they'd lined up for a trust fall, and the boy she loved stood behind her. She could hear his sharp intake of breath behind her. She tucked her arms into her chest and fell. She felt like a stone and then felt the bulk of his body catching her, quickly, efficiently. She could feel the slat of his ribs against her back, his fingers in the flesh of her shoulders. She felt radiant with touch. This sometimes felt like the happiest she'd been in her life.

3. You've got to put yourself out there more.

Were you there at the wedding of their ex last week when they popped out of a wedding cake wearing their phone number as a sash? This person invented putting themselves out there.

She's grown tired of dating apps, weddings. She doesn't want to log in to see if anyone has matched her, has found those carefully curated photos appealing and said hello at eleven p.m., invited her over. She knows it shouldn't be so, but each failed conversation, each match that doesn't happen, feels like a fresh cut on her thin psyche. She reads about women who go on dates, have frequent sex, but she can't bring herself to it. Most nights, she curls into a ball on her couch, hugs her knees and watches television.

She's tired of standing at parties, at the weddings of friend after friend, looking at the place settings, so perfect, the arbor of grapes. She drinks too much wine and pees frequently. Even at her best, when she's joyously dancing to every typical wedding song, spinning around the room like a top, she can't help but wonder, in the quiet, if her person is there, somewhere, searching, too. She looks and looks at all the places the light goes, but everyone is with someone else, not looking at her.

4. Are you seeing anyone right now?

Of course they aren't seeing anyone right now, or they'd have changed their relationship status on Facebook, they'd have Instagram'd out photos of them having brunch at a trendy spot in that newly gentrified neighborhood and sent you a Christmas card talking about the trials and travails of their first month together, including a particularly troublesome battle with a tree stand and a misshapen Douglas fir. There would be numerous pictures of an orange cat.

She saw someone for a while recently, a friend of a friend. She'd tracked his number down, introduced herself, all the things she wouldn't normally do. It felt like having a tooth pulled without Novocain. On dates, he seemed happy but distant. They'd gone to a restaurant that overlooked a garden, peonies, foxglove, snapdragons. They'd talked about their childhoods. She'd shared something about her mother's distance growing up, the way she'd always felt alone as a child, as though everything was dependent on her. She started crying. She'd never told anyone about her mother. Two weeks later, he stopped texting, he disappeared like the fog that burns off over the bay, as if there had been nothing there at all. Would there ever be something, she thought, as she ate dinner alone while watching a rerun of an old show she'd loved as a teenager.

5. The right one is just around the corner.

Nah. They just checked around the corner. They saw a squirrel digging through bits of trash and finding a shiny button, and a blue sedan parked poorly in a spot. There is nothing much more to see around the next corner.

On a walk, she rounds the corner and sees a group of men gathering at a bus stop. She walks quickly, head down, hoping they won't say something to her, a feeling that she carries with her, not just when men are gathering at bus stops but everywhere. She wishes she could shrink her desires down into a small shell. She'd take her desire out in the backyard and bury it like a squirrel does an acorn in winter, losing track of it forever. Instead, it blooms within her; its thorns leave marks on the inside of her stomach.

6. Have you read *Eat, Pray, Love*?

Of course they have. But they are savvy enough to understand that underlying the message of eat, get religion, get a man, is that meeting a man is still the raison d'etre for a journey of self-discovery, which doesn't even begin to get at the inherent class conflicts and problematizing of cultures as monolithic entities in which one can only eat, pray, or love.

She reads a book about love and tosses it away. She's not drawn to those sorts of stories. She doesn't seem to like any stories of late and certainly not her own, which she is reminded of each morning, in that quiet moment in the shower. This is life. What she's seeking in books is an answer to her own life, thirty-seven, single, sad. But she can't find a writer or a story that exactly matches her own, the lonely childhood, the cutting, and at times, the joy. She thinks of joining a book club, of taking up running again, of anything that will reorient her life, which she is constantly examining and never changing. She feels like an observer, an anthropologist of her own life. I do this, then that. But the catalog continues day after day, and there is no one to assemble the results and make meaning of them. Maybe she should date a statistician.

7. Have you considered colonizing Mars?

Everyone has considered colonizing Mars. Everybody knows about island syndrome. Imagine what ship syndrome is like? No one is leaving that ship single. No one.

Once, years ago now, she'd been involved with someone who colonized her. They used to wander the labyrinth of streets at night, lamplight pooling on corners. And as they walked, they talked of therapy, of childhood, of dreams. She felt each time they talked as if another piece of her was slipping away until she was entirely his, fragment by fragment, like a piece of dust, slowly reassembling into a belt around a planet. She orbited him.

He had a wife in Russia and a child. He was in her city on a research grant, studying particle physics. Once, before he left, they'd gone camping at the beach and sat beneath the blue moon and watched the waves stamp at the shore. This, too, was the happiest moment of her life.

8. Have you thought about the tax deductions?

Of course, they stay up late at night on midrange comforters purchased from Sleepy's, with their glasses resting on an IKEA nightstand from the Hemnes line, brown-black, thinking about all the line items they are missing out on by being single.

She shops at Trader Joe's to save money, picking up snacks, peanut butter pretzels, chocolate-covered almonds, chocolate-covered raisins, two baguettes. At home, she eats them in a rush, stares out the window at an empty street below as the rose of desire blooms inside her. She can feel its petals at her esophagus.

9. Have you considered going to Europe, taking up poetry or painting and riding around on trains?

She wants to go to Spain, as she did as a child, wants to take no language courses, so she can only have rudimentary conversations about the weather. And when people ask about her, how she's doing, she won't know how to say anything but OK. She wants to tell everyone that she meets that she is fine, OK. She doesn't want to be able to articulate all the things that she feels, the convulsions of emotions, the sadness at her parents, her love life. She thinks, maybe, just maybe, if she doesn't have the words to describe it, if all she can say over and over is OK, then perhaps the words will make it true.

She signs up for a class where you drink wine and paint, hoping to meet someone. In class, she starts to paint, but feels it going poorly, her painting; it is abstract instead of real, and she walks out of the building into a warm breeze. There are gray clouds hung between two buildings. She stands like that for a few minutes, breathing in and out, hoping that someone will come out of the class and talk to her, ask her if she's OK. She wonders if she radiates loneliness.

10. It's great being alone.

She doesn't think it's great being alone. She's read things about the difference between loneliness and simply being alone. She's lonely often, she knows, and can never seem to aim the slight cuts to the place where it hurts most. She thinks of being alone for the next forty years, and time is like a field of wheat, flowing in the breeze, acres, and acres of time, to sleep, to drink, to eat, to dream. Some dreams feel more real than life, she thinks, as the dark shadow of a bird flies across her window, hidden by the blinds, a reflection from Plato's cave.

The man she'd known returns on a second fellowship, and this time, though in every other way he is the same as the first time, he has no wife, no child, is wholly available to her. When he tells a joke, he touches her shoulder with his left hand, as if pulling her into it. His eyes wrinkle slightly as he looks at her—what a world. They drive out again to the beach, talking of their lives the whole ride. She feels so safe. The two of them camp on the beach beneath the blue moon, the sea of stars, and they hold each other tightly, while overhead the galaxy swims on, like a fish caught in the wide net of the universe.

A TRANSLATOR'S NOTE: THE DEFINITIVE EDITION

The translation, admittedly, has a number of defects, which are at least partially attributable to the fact that I cannot read Italian. And yet, I have tried when possible to capture the pure essence of what the esteemed writer's language probably meant. In certain passages, I'd humbly argue that my translation surpasses those of all three prior translations of the author's work. Those translators had at their disposal only a working knowledge of Italian and small academic grants that allowed them to spend countless hours in dim libraries, parsing his words and trying to account for all nuances of meaning before settling on the correct word, while I, being slightly older than all three, have the great and unattainable thing of which they can only dream.

I saw the great writer once at a book shop in Venice. It was near the end of his life, and the skin sagged from his face like cloth from a sail. He was across the room from me, behind old leather-bound volumes, and a globe, which showed an outsized version of Italy. His great white beard and unkempt hair, falling to near his shoulders, made him immediately identifiable. He was, this great man, leaning in very close to hear the words of a very beautiful woman, but I could see the twinkle in his eye, the soul not yet at rest. From that moment

I have gathered all of my inspiration for the text, and though it may differ occasionally in form, content, and certain items of the plot, I confess to you reader that no one knew him better than I and that I can confidently declare this work the definitive translation.

ACKNOWLEDGEMENTS

Apt: "When We Lived by the Sea"

The Broadkill Review: "Forty Days"

Catamaran Literary Reader: "Something Miraculous"

Cease, Cows: "The Earth in Its Flight" and "In the Garden"

December Magazine: "Maybe This Time"

Eclectica: "Being and Time"

Emerge Literary Journal: "What I'd Forgive"

Eunoia Review: "Migrations"

Fiction Southeast: "It Sings"

Flash Fiction Press: "The Nature of Time"

Gravel: "The Note"

Hobart: "It Rained Laughter"

JMWW: "Dream Mother"

Literary Orphans: "Come Winter" and "A Retraction"

Microfiction Monday Magazine: "Across Town"

Moon City Review: "The Space Between Us"

No Contact Mag: "Mother's Garden"

Necessary Fiction: "Of Lakes and Swans"

OxMag: "River Walk"

Pithead Chapel: "A Preface to the Third Edition"

Prism Review: "Waking Dreams"

Redivider: "Courtesy of *Cosmopolitan*: 24 Big Bang Sex Tips"

Sierra Nevada Review: "One Person Away From You" and "Things She's Tired of Hearing"

Storychord: "A Woman's Life: An Abridged Version"

The Threepenny Review: "A Translator's Note: The Definitive Edition"

Tin House: "Everyone in This Story"

Whiskey Paper: "That Summer"

Witness: "The Arrival of the Sea"

"A Translator's Note" also appeared in *The Best American Poetry 2018*.

MOON CITY
SHORT FICTION AWARD
WINNERS

2014
Cate McGowan
True Places Never Are

2015
Laura Hendrix Ezell
A Record of Our Debts

2016
Michelle Ross
There's So Much They Haven't Told You

2017
Kim Magowan
Undoing

2018
Amanda Marbais
Claiming a Body

2019
Pablo Piñero Stillmann
*Our Brains and the Brains
of Miniature Sharks*

2020
Andrew Bertaina
One Person Away From You

CPSIA information can be obtained
at www.ICGtesting.com
Printed in the USA
JSHW032122220522
26116JS00003B/17